"I Presume You're Larry's Fiancée."

Anne didn't know what to reply. She'd had next to nothing to drink, yet she felt giddy. Music going to her head, she guessed, and fatigue. But there was something else, something overpoweringly masculine that seemed to radiate from Evan Forrester. She felt nervous, yet the warmth of his body as he guided her through the languorously slow music was having the effect of strong wine coursing through her system. She didn't want the dance to end, yet her conscience was disturbed. She shouldn't be enjoying this moment. There was something wrong with feeling this tremulous, this . . . this *excited*.

JANE CONVERSE

is one of Silhouette's more prolific authors, having published more than sixty novels under various pseudonyms. She makes her home in California, but has travelled extensively. Her recent trips include Hawaii, Mexico and Japan.

Dear Reader,

Silhouette Special Editions are an exciting new line of contemporary romances from Silhouette Books. Special Editions are written specifically for our readers who want a story with greater romantic detail.

Special Editions have all the elements you've enjoyed in Silhouette Romances and *more*. These stories concentrate on romance in a longer, more realistic and sophisticated way, and they feature greater sensual detail.

I hope you enjoy this book and all the wonderful romances from Silhouette. We welcome any suggestions or comments and invite you to write to us at the address below.

Elaine Shelley
Silhouette Books
PO Box 703
Dunton Green
Sevenoaks
Kent
TN13 2YE

JANE CONVERSE
Paradise Postponed

Silhouette Special Edition

Published by Silhouette Books

Copyright © 1981 by Silhouette Books,
a Simon & Schuster Division of Gulf &
Western Corporation

Map by Tony Ferrara

First printing 1982

British Library C.I.P.

Converse, Jane
    Paradise postponed.—(Silhouette special edition)
    I. Title
    813´.54[F]   PS3553.0544

    ISBN 0 340 28583 4

Printed and bound in Great Britain for
Hodder and Stoughton Paperbacks, a
division of Hodder and Stoughton Ltd.,
Mill Road, Dunton Green, Sevenoaks,
Kent (Editorial Office: 47 Bedford
Square, London, WC1 3DP) by
Richard Clay (The Chaucer Press) Ltd.,
Bungay, Suffolk

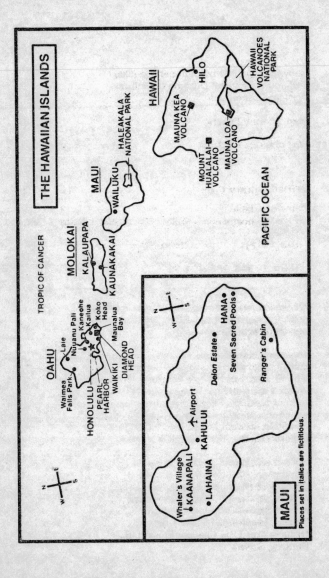

Chapter One

*E*very once in a while, as the giant jet winged its way across the vast expanse between Chicago and Los Angeles, then as they had made the five-and-one-half-hour flight from Los Angeles to Honolulu, Anne Beal had cast a still-shy, wondering glance at the man beside her. Now, during the short flight from Oahu to Maui, Anne had stopped blushing when Larry Delon returned her smile and patted her hand. But the wonderment of it all had not ceased. He was *the* Lawrence Delon III. She was wearing a monstrous diamond ring on her left hand. And she was on her way to the tropical paradise where Larry's family had one of their luxurious homes, apprehensive about meeting his socially prominent mother, brother, and sister-in-law, still not quite able to believe that she was going to the Delon estate on Maui to plan their wedding!

When the other young women in the secretarial pool at the prestigious brokerage firm of Delon and Withrow had admired Anne's ring and wondered enviously how lucky any girl could get, Anne had wondered, too. She had been fresh out of secretarial school only six months before when she had been hired by the LaSalle Street firm. Most of the other female employees were Chicago bred, knowledgeable about buying chic clothing when the elegant Michigan Boulevard shops held seasonal sales, and well acquainted with the city's restaurants and theaters, art galleries and boutiques, discos and smart supper clubs. Their savoir-faire was a constant reminder to Anne that she must appear to them as a naïve, small-town bumpkin. Yet they had not been snobbish or unfriendly. In fact, several of her co-workers had made a project out of transforming the newcomer from a small-town girl into a modern sophisticate, at least in appearance.

Anne's long auburn hair had been cut and expertly styled. She had learned that one smartly understated suit was worth a dozen of the inexpensive little dresses that had composed her wardrobe. And she had learned to make the most of her slim-waisted figure, good legs, and blue-green eyes. She had never thought of herself as particularly attractive. Yet within a few months, Anne was beginning to like what she saw in the mirror, and with the change in her appearance came a new self-confidence. No one, she guessed, would know merely from looking at her that she was the daughter of a dour, strict bookkeeper, that she had been her father's housekeeper since her mother had died when Anne was thirteen, that dates and school dances had been dreamed of but not permitted, or that during her secretarial training she had been too tired from paying her own tuition by working as a night-shift waitress to enjoy a social life.

But Anne had learned her skills well. When, after only three months at Delon and Withrow, she had been moved up to the executive offices, none of the other typists or file clerks had been envious or surprised. There had been a small after-hours party to celebrate Anne's promotion, a comparatively exciting event after the endless evenings at home alone watching television, which were broken only by an occasional movie with Joan and Peggy from the accounting department. But there had been no dates, nor even the hope of male interest around the office. If anything, the situation in Anne's new department was more discouraging: the executives were either old or married; usually both. There was only one exception: the scion of the Delon clan himself. His grandfather had established the firm but it was his dedication and financial wizardry that accounted for the firm's continuing growth and success. Certainly he was not to be thought of as a romantic prospect.

Yet there had been, on the rare occasions when Anne encountered Mr. Delon in the plush reception room or in the elevators, a polite smile, then a subdued gleam of interest, and finally, on an evening when Anne had voluntarily stayed to work overtime, a personal visit to her desk and a compliment on her "outstanding performance."

Lawrence Delon was not exceptionally handsome nor was he unattractive. He wore his hand-tailored suits in the manner of a man who has never worn anything else, yet without flair; any show of flashiness was frowned upon in these conservative environs. He was of medium height, slender and wiry, his features finely symmetrical, his nose and chin a trifle sharp. Although it was known that he was only in his early thirties, Lawrence Delon's light-brown, short-clipped hair was tinged with gray at the temples, an effect that added to his aristocratic air. He was unfailingly soft-spoken. And it was in that subdued Ivy League–accented voice that he astounded Anne Beal one morning by asking if she were free the next evening for dinner and the opening of a new musical.

Anne had stammered an acceptance, spending the day correcting nervous and untypical errors, wondering why the invitation had been extended. She had seen Mr. Delon's picture in the daily papers, escorting scintillating debutantes to charity balls, attending swank parties in North Shore mansions and fabled penthouses. Would he come for her at the drab little apartment she was now sharing with her two new-found friends from accounting? Would he be embarrassed by her naïveté or by what she wore? And what *should* she wear?

All the panic had been unnecessary, all the questions academic. Lawrence Delon's poise made him comfortable under any circumstances, and his ease had quickly erased Anne's tension. During their dinner at one of the better hotel dining rooms, he had chatted in a casual, impersonal manner about subjects that were not beyond Anne's understanding. They had liked the same films. They had both spent a Saturday afternoon at the Art Institute and had concluded that the sculptor whose work was on exhibit, while technically gifted, was probably thumbing his nose at the public. And although Lawrence Delon was not given to hilarious laughter and Anne was still not relaxed enough to lead the way, they had been able to smile at each other across the table about the waiter's pompous attitude.

It had been an eventful evening only because it had happened at all. Lawrence Delon was a *millionaire,* for heaven's sake, well educated, well traveled, almost a legend in financial circles, his lineage strictly blue blood. It seemed incredible that he should be asking Anne to call him Larry; even more incredible that his good-night kiss was gentle and respectful. He had not, as Anne had feared, asked her out to satisfy his need for a temporary playmate.

Even more incredible was Larry's second

invitation a few days later, and the next and the next. In a matter of weeks, his kisses became less brotherly and more ardent, though there was always a certain polite reserve in his manner. He was not aloof; it was simply that he never lost his exceptional poise.

And then there had been the night when Anne's roommates had discreetly gone to stay with suburban relatives and she had dared to invite Larry Delon to dinner. Let him see how simply she lived, Anne decided. She would be totally honest with him. No escargot or breast of veal tonight. He knew exactly how much she was earning and what she could afford. Let him see what could be done with ground round, brown rice and an imagination born out of necessity.

Larry had marveled over the dinner. The wine he had brought had been appropriately unpretentious. And Anne had told him about herself, her humble background, even admitting that her social life in the big city had hardly been exciting. She had expected him to respond with a pitying glance. Instead, Larry had said, "You're so honest and refreshing, Anne. You spoke, earlier, of never having met anyone like me. Please accept this as a compliment, dear. I haven't even come close to knowing anyone like you."

The Pinot Chardonnay was almost all gone when their conversation had turned to the personnel at Delon and Withrow and then to the ambitions of some of the younger members of the staff. Most of the already married male employees were scrambling up the junior executive ladder, planning a career in stocks and bonds. With one exception, the women were hoping to meet a prospective husband.

"And you?" Larry asked.

"I don't know," Anne said. "I don't think I'm qualified to manage anyone's portfolio." She smiled. "Not unless it has a handle on it and I can move it from one end of the room to the other."

Larry laughed, delighted with her honest reply.

"And I don't suppose I can aspire to being your secretary. Miss Paget's so perfect for the job. So efficient, so . . . almost like an institution."

"And with absolutely no intention of ever retiring, fortunately for me." Larry reached into his jacket pocket. "And if she did, you'd be the last person I'd want to replace her."

Anne looked over at him questioningly. "I wouldn't be *that* unqualified, would I?"

"No, but you'd be entirely too distracting. I wouldn't be able to keep my mind on my work. Our clients would desert us in droves." Larry extracted a small box from his pocket. "And, in any case, I have better plans for you, Anne."

His words, his expression, the size of the box in his hand forced the air from Anne's lungs. He couldn't be thinking, he couldn't be about to say . . .

But he did say it. "I love you, Anne. I would like to marry you."

He said it simply, almost . . . almost *efficiently*, Anne thought. The way he might propose a stock transaction to an old established client. Yet the question had been asked, and the ring box was opened to reveal a diamond that glittered, enormous, under the lamplight. And he was holding the ring in his hand, his eyes gentle, almost imploring, and yet reflecting his usual confidence. What was it someone had once said about him? "When L.D. goes after something, he goes at it knowing he's going to get it."

Later, Anne might stop to wonder if the romantic aura surrounding those moments had not been created by her own hunger for love. But his kiss was warm and meaningful; his arms around Anne firm and reassuring. "I want to take care of you for the rest of your life," Larry murmured against her ear. "I adore you, darling. I'm going to make you the happiest girl in the world."

She did not remember giving him a verbal reply. She had responded to his kiss, she had let Larry slip the diamond on the significant ring finger of her left hand, and, more dazed than ecstatic, she had listened to Larry talk with a strangely boyish enthusiasm about their future together. They would travel, they would vacation in the Delon family's bayside home in Nassau, they would combine his annual business trip to Europe with sightseeing, Anne would never lack for any material thing her heart desired.

It was not until the news raced through the offices of Delon and Withrow that it fully penetrated Anne's consciousness; she was going to be married to a millionaire, a man whose name was undoubtedly inscribed in the social register, a man who was closely tied to his distinguished family. Amid congratulations from her co-workers, and phrases like, "Oh boy, have you ever got it *made!*" Anne began to emerge from her bewildered euphoric state to realize that she had made the most serious commitment of her life. And when Larry outlined his plan for their wedding, even setting the date in June, two months following, a panic set in. His family—would they accept her? Did they know that she was a nobody with the most humble background imaginable? What if they didn't think she was good enough for Larry?

Larry's responses to these questions were unhesitating. How could they not love the woman he had chosen to marry? He was a grown man, a responsible adult, capable of making his own choices. He wanted Anne to be his wife. She was charming and lovable. Who could *avoid* loving her?

Yet, with the offices of Larry's firm behind

her, the bridal shower given by the office staff an exciting memory, a wardrobe provided by Larry as his engagement present checked through to Maui, Anne could not help asking herself one meaningful question. Did she really *love* this man who was going to make—had already made—such a radical change in her life?

Glancing at him, Anne was rewarded with a kindly smile. He was thoughtful, he was generous, he was unfailingly kind. Since he had placed the ring on her finger, Larry had not let a day go by during which he had not told Anne that he loved her. Several times, when he hesitated afterward, as though encouraging a response in kind from Anne, she had said, "I love you, too." It disturbed her that the echoed words sometimes sounded mechanical and that she did not quicken at the sight of him or feel her heart beating faster at the sound of his voice when he phoned her to make arrangements for their evening dates. But these were the reactions invented by the writers of Victorian romances, Anne told herself. They were the symptoms of puppy love, more appropriate to starry-eyed high school girls. Theirs was a solid relationship, based on . . . based on what? Trust, respect, mature judgment. It was not a fleeting physical attraction or an exaggerated storybook kind of romance in which bells rang and whistles blew. A powerful, logical, important man who knew his own mind had chosen to share his life with her. "I hope you know how lucky you are," one of the stenos at the office had said. And Anne had replied, "Oh, I do. I really do." She felt that way now; loved, secure, fortunate. And who knew what it was really like to be insanely in love?

Chapter Two

$\mathcal{A}$ white Porsche was waiting for them at the airport near Kahului, their point of arrival on the island of Maui. It might be an interminable wait for their luggage, Larry explained. "Bertie Knowles will pick it up in the station wagon," he said. "I'm anxious to get home and have the family fall in love with you, as I have."

Larry must have sensed her apprehension. Would the white linen suit she had chosen for the plane trip be too simple, too dressy, too wrinkled? Was she wearing too much makeup or not enough? Anne felt Larry's right hand close over her fingers, giving them a reassuring squeeze. And then she was lost in admiring the beautiful coastline, the emerald and turquoise waters of the bay, then the exotic tropical verdure that edged the twisting road. A sharp turn brought them in sight of a crystal-clear waterfall tumbling into a fern-surrounded blue pool. Sunlight on the mist from this cascade had bisected it with a glorious rainbow. Anne almost forgot the meeting that lay ahead, so lost was she in the beauty of the paradise through which Larry was driving her.

She must have sounded incredibly naïve in her enthusiasm. "That's a split-leaf philodendron! I had a small one in my apartment that cost *twenty dollars*. That one . . . oh, look, hundreds of them . . . climbing up trees! They must be forty feet tall!"

"I can't tell you what your little-girl enthusiasm does for me," Larry said. He took another sharp turn in the road, then leaned over to kiss Anne's forehead. "I've gotten terribly blasé. What a joy it's going to be to show you the world and to see it through your eyes, your beautiful, beautiful eyes."

His words stilled the queasiness inside her, but Anne was unprepared for the opulence of the Delon estate. The house itself, a two-story modern affair constructed of redwood, fieldstone, and glass, sat on a promontory overlooking the blue Pacific. Anne had expected something staid and traditional, in keeping with the conservative family name, but the structure was almost aggressively new looking, obviously the triumph of some noted contemporary designer. It was reached from the road by a short white gravel driveway that was bordered by an explosion of bright-blooming shrubs. Hibiscus, Larry explained. A profusion of purple and orange bougainvillaea spilled from long planter boxes on the second story. An emerald green, pristinely manicured lawn separated the house, on one side, from two tennis courts. On the other side, a winding path led through a carefully cultivated jungle to a fieldstone patio studded with huge white urns filled with brightly blossoming flowers. Gaily striped umbrellas shaded a scattering of white wrought-iron and glass tables. All of this color served as a frame for a swimming pool that had been formed to resemble a woodland pond. Huge lava rock boulders and palm trees completed the stunning effect. And just beyond the pool, framed by a stand of dark green, scarlet flowering trees, the ocean's brilliant blue vied with the aquamarine color of the man-made pool. It was breathtaking, not only in its loveliness but in its grandeur. Only in movies had Anne seen anything that compared with this setting. And this was not the only Delon estate. It was one of several that Larry had casually mentioned.

A tiny dark-haired maid with a shy smile opened the door for them, greeting Larry with a pleased smile. "Oh, Mr. Delon! How good it is to see you!" Larry had told Anne that with the exception of the butler and the housekeeper, all of the servents were of Filipino origin. This pretty young maid was introduced as Amalia. She looked at Anne with something like awe, but she was not too impressed to smile once more.

Larry gave her instructions to see that their luggage was sent for immediately, then asked, "Where is everybody?"

Before the maid could reply, a shrill, theatrical female voice was heard saying, "Oh, he

did make an earlier plane! Lawrence, darling,
you're becoming entirely too predictable."

Anne stood behind Larry in the entry hall,
turning her eyes from the glass-enclosed
atrium to see a tall thin woman approaching,
her arms extended so that the flowing sleeves
of what appeared to be a long hand-printed
dashiki created a butterfly effect. She knew
from Larry that his mother was approaching
sixty, yet the slender figure, the smartly
coiffed silver-white hair, the unique wrought
silver dangle earrings and the armload of
hand-wrought silver bracelets were hardly
calculated to give a matronly impression.
Anne caught a glimpse of an almost wrinkle-
free face and an ivory-smooth complexion
tanned to serve as a perfect background for
heavily made-up eyes that managed to look
sharp and bright in spite of their pale blue
color. Mrs. Delon's sharp nose and chin established her as Larry's mother, and she wore
the same proprietary air with which Larry
unconsciously walked through the offices of
Delon and Withrow. Larry was carefully em-
braced, his cheek pecked with the barest hint
of contact, and then Anne was presented to
Mrs. Delon.

Anne, too, was greeted with a rather dramatic but cautious hug. Mrs. Delon's kiss was
aimed at the air, and Anne noticed that she
was being simultaneously surveyed by those
almost colorless eyes. She was examined
quickly but expertly, as Larry's mother said,
"Welcome to our little aerie, my dear." A

sweeping motion of her hands indicated her son. "Lawrence, I would never have dreamed you had access to the dormitory at Miss Brookley's."

Larry smiled, then explained to Anne that Miss Brookley's was a finishing school in suburban Chicago; his mother was commenting, in her own facetious way, on Anne's youthful appearance.

"I shouldn't think you'd have to explain," Mrs. Delon said.

Anne gave Larry an uncomfortable glance. She had never heard of the exclusive school. She felt quite "unfinished." Certainly she had not been a student there.

Mrs. Delon didn't wait for responses. She turned abruptly. "Your rooms are ready, but there's no point in going up until Bertie fetches your luggage. You *did* send him along, didn't you, Lawrence?" Again, she didn't wait for a reply. "The clan's gathered out on the lanai. Surely you're dying for a drink?"

Larry's mother did not wait for answers to her questions because they were not really questions at all. They were statements. She projected a somewhat showy charm with a cool, imperious undertone that told you she expected things done her way. Perhaps I'm being too hasty in judging her, Anne thought. Larry linked his arm through hers, locking his fingers with Anne's as though he sensed that she needed his moral support. They followed Mrs. Delon through a spacious tile-floored room furnished with groupings of white wicker furniture, glass tables footed by dramatic arrangements of bleached driftwood and a veritable forest of enormous green ferns. Late-afternoon sunshine illuminated another glass-walled area just beyond the living room, and Anne noted that this indoor-outdoor area resembled nothing more than a tropical hothouse. A white rattan bar dominated one solid wall; the rest of the room afforded a spectacular view of the sea.

There were three other people waiting to be introduced. One, a rather paunchy, red-faced man who hadn't the slightest resemblance to Larry or to Mrs. Delon, lumbered to his feet and was introduced as Larry's brother, Warren. Anne felt a slight revulsion at the contact of his plump warm hand as Warren greeted her with a laconic, "Welcome to the family conclave, dear." Anne noted that he had not let go of the highball glass in his hand and that his words were carelessly slurred together. She was grateful that she had not been subjected to a welcoming kiss by the flabby, wet lips. How could he possibly be Larry's brother?

Neither of the other people present rose from her lounge chair as Larry did the honors. They were two women, one a spectacularly beautiful blonde, more deeply tanned than Mrs. Delon. Her eyes, also blue, were of a more intense shade that bordered on violet. Her hair was long and parted in the center, somewhat windblown but attractive. She looked athletic, energetic, and so casually

dressed in faded denim shorts and a plain
spaghetti-strapped top that Anne's immediate
impression was one of wealth. Inez Carruthers, who was apparently a house guest,
looked so securely affluent that she could
have bought her clothes at a thrift shop and
still exuded the smell of money. But her smile
seemed cordial enough, as did the wave of her
long fingers as she said, "Hi." Just "hi," nothing more, before she returned her concentra-
tion to her nearly empty martini glass.

One could easily have overlooked the other
woman in a crowd. She was petite, rather
birdlike, perhaps about thirty. She had a quiet
voice that somehow matched her mousy-
brown hair. Pulled back in a ponytail, her hair
provided a rather harsh and unflattering
framework for ordinary and not perfectly
symmetrical features. But her large hazel
eyes glowed a warm welcome and her smile
was perfection itself. She extended her hand
and pressed Anne's warmly as she welcomed
her to the family circle. She was Warren's
wife, a Delon by marriage as Anne would
soon be. Her name was Veronica.

Anne was invited to sit down in one of the
tropical-print-covered patio chairs and Larry
insisted upon going to the bar and fixing
daiquiris for Anne and for himself. The conversation Anne had dreaded hardly materialized; it was more a monologue by Mrs. Delon.
Would they care for a light snack or something
more substantial? Neither? Well, marvelous.
There was a luau planned for tonight. The

Carpenters were on the island for a week—
"Larry, you do remember the Carpenters? Up
to their ears building condominiums here and
on the Big Island. Rentals, if you can imagine
anything more dreadful. They've turned our
beautiful Lahaina into another Miami Beach.
It's simply crawling with package-deal tourists in tacky rayon aloha shirts and the inevi-
table matching muumuus." She rattled on,
sprightly and, she must be certain, youthfully
amusing, probably relishing the destruction of
Anne's preconceived image of her. Yet Anne
was not unaware of a carefully barbed snob-
bishness. "I told Edith Carpenter, 'Money is
one thing, darling, but think of being listed in
the register as *innkeepers!*'"

Larry listened to this recital with a benign
smile on his face. The others looked faintly
bored, only glancing up from their drinks
once in a while to give the stranger in their
midst a subtle inspection. No one asked about
their trip. Was that a lack of interest or did
they do so much jet-setting that the three
flights, from Chicago to Los Angeles, then to
Honolulu and finally, the shorter hop to Maui,
were insignificant events, like walking to the
corner newsstand. Still, it was a relief to have
Mrs. Delon going on and on, mostly about
herself—her friends, her parties, her homes,
her servants, her family's prestige. It saved
Anne the discomfort of being interviewed,
something she had foolishly dreaded.

It was probably foolish, also, to look at Inez
Carruthers and imagine that she would have

been Mrs. Delon's choice of a wife for Larry. Inez certainly showed little interest in him. And when Larry made himself comfortable beside Anne, taking her hand in his, she found herself relaxing. She was in an incredibly beautiful place, without a worry in the world, seated close to a man who loved her. She was going to marry Larry, not his family. And, thus far, they had done nothing to make her feel unwelcome in their midst.

They watched a spectacular sunset before Mrs. Delon announced that it was time to change for the luau that had been called for eight thirty, poolside. Everyone rose, languidly, as though performing a boring duty. As they left the lanai, Veronica touched Anne's forearm and whispered in her ear, "You managed far better than I did, honey. But, then, Millicent knew that Warren was no prize."

Anne threw her an appreciative smile, though she wasn't quite sure she understood. Millicent. That would be Mrs. Delon, of course. Millicent Withrow Delon; her late father had been a partner in the Delon's brokerage firm. Yes, and Veronica must have felt the same apprehension in being introduced to her when she became Warren's prospective bride. And indeed, Warren was hardly a "prize." From Anne's brief observation of him, he seemed content to lounge around and consume liquor. A few desultory comments had made it clear that he had no interest in the family business. Nor, for that matter, in his wife. He and Larry were as different as it was possible for brothers to be.

Larry escorted Anne to the guest room that had been reserved for her. Once he had shown her inside the airy, beautifully furnished room, he told her that everyone had adored her, as he had known that they would.

Anne managed a smile. "You mean I passed the first test?"

"You more than passed the only one that counts," Larry said, kissing her on the temple and then, lightly, on the lips. "I love you." He gave her a gentle, almost brotherly hug.

Why was it always so difficult for her to say, "I love you, too"? Sometimes Larry was like a stranger in Anne's eyes—still the important, unapproachable Mr. Delon who occupied the mahogany-paneled office to which minor functionaries at Delon and Withrow did not have access. She had to keep reminding herself that this was the man she was going to marry. She had to look at the ring on her finger to confirm her reason for being in this lovely place: Larry's mother was going to help her make plans for a wedding!

As Larry was leaving the room for his own, across the hall, he asked if Anne was up to a party. "If you're tired, dear, I'm sure everyone will understand."

She *was* tired, but she knew sleep would be impossible. Besides, she didn't want Larry thinking that she couldn't keep up with the social pace to which he was accustomed.

"Miss my first luau? I wouldn't think of it," Anne said. "Except . . . Larry?"

In the doorway, he turned and smiled. "I know. You're going to ask me what to wear."

Anne nodded. "I don't . . . own anything Hawaiian."

"We'll take care of that tomorrow," Larry said. "And, believe me, Mother will give you ten points for going against the grain. She wouldn't be caught dead in a Hawaiian print. Unless she was in Cairo or Acapulco. She'll demonstrate her security by wearing something she picked up in Guatemala. *You*, dearest, wear any colorful thing you please." Anne had followed him to the door. He chucked her under the chin, his eyes bright with approval. "Whatever you wear, you'll be the loveliest wahine who ever decided that she doesn't like poi. I'll knock on your door in, say, an hour."

Alone, Anne explored the room. The huge walk-in closet already held her wardrobe. Evidently one of the maids had unpacked and put all of her belongings away. Yes, her makeup kit sat on the white dressing table, her lingerie had been neatly arranged in its drawers. And the huge bathroom, tiled in pale green, was stocked with everything a house guest could ask for. *House guest*. Would she ever reach a stage when she felt that she was more than just a visitor in this incredible house? *Mrs. Lawrence Delon*. Anne shook her head in wonderment. *Anne Delon*. Mistress of all she surveyed? She repeated the name out loud. *Anne Delon*. It sounded foreign, and she almost laughed. But there was a strange, disquieting heaviness inside her as she undressed and stepped into the shower. Tiredness, she decided. There was no other explanation for the feeling that something heavy was weighing against her chest, making it hard for her to breathe, making her feel as though . . . as though she wanted to *cry!*

She felt better after the shower and was almost in a gala mood as she slipped into the bare-shouldered teal cotton that Larry's secretary had helped her select during one of their shopping sprees. A long dress wouldn't be inappropriate, she decided. And the crinkly fabric was hardly Hawaiian; Mrs. Delon would approve of that. Anne smiled at the quaint snobbery. A Delon had to be different, but not *too* different. Would she ever learn all the rules? More important, did she want to? Larry had make it a point, repeatedly, to tell her that he loved her for her unpretentiousness. She wasn't going to be an imitation of his mother. Anne lifted her chin in the air as she brushed her casually cut hair. She was Anne Beal, daughter of a bookkeeper from a small coal-mining town. And she was going to be exactly who she was. If she'd owned a bright yellow muumuu splashed with trite red hibiscus flowers, she would have worn it tonight.

When he knocked on her door exactly an hour later, Larry approved. He always approved. He always said exactly the right thing, Anne thought. To clients, employees,

family members, to her. Always polite. Sometimes—sometimes, even when he was flattering her, she thought of him as a bit . . .
No, that wasn't fair. He wasn't dull. He
was all a woman could hope for. She had
never before seen him in anything as casual
as the white designer jeans and simple yellow
and green sport shirt he was wearing. Away
from the office, in this informal setting, she
might get to know him as a different person;
younger in spirit, more relaxed, maybe even
more . . . *fun*.

Dozens of blazing torches had transformed
the patio into an exciting setting for the Hawaiian feast. Some of the guests had already
arrived when Larry and Anne came downstairs. Apparently additional help had been
hired; there seemed to be aloha-shirted waiters everywhere, including two behind a portable bar that had been set up since Anne's
arrival and her first view of the pool area.
Anne found herself being introduced to people
Larry had evidently known for a long time,
most of them his mother's age or older,
though there was a sprinkling of tanned
young people who looked as though they
might just have come off the tennis court or a
boat and hadn't bothered to change clothes.

Mrs. Delon's shrill laughter was heard from
time to time, but she seemed to be occupied
with guests on the far end of the patio. The
young people spoke of tennis and yachting, the
older crowd discussed golf scores. Few people
commented on Larry's engagement, although

he introduced Anne to everyone as his fiancée. It was as though the forthcoming wedding had not been announced to anyone. Anne
did not feel out of place, yet neither did she
feel at home. She was simply *there*, exchanging polite banalities with people who held
little interest for her, though that, too, was
unfair. She had had a long day. And the air
was so warm and balmy, so caressing, that
after the first mai tai, she wanted nothing
more than to curl up in one of the lounge
chairs and drift off to sleep.

A five-piece band that alternated between
Hawaiian music and pop tunes played from a
palm-frond-covered stand. A few people
danced; most stood around nursing drinks.
Anne noticed that Inez Carruthers was the
center of one group that sat dangling bare feet
in the water at the shallow end of the swimming pool. Warren Delon was slouched in a
lounge chair, swirling a tall drink and looking
as though he would rather be elsewhere. His
wife seemed to be busy supervising the serving of canapés and consulting with the Hawaiians who were in charge of the imu, the
earthen pit in which, Larry had explained, a
huge roast pig had been cooking slowly all day
in its bed of hot stones, taro, and ti leaves.

As more guests poured onto the patio, one
elderly gentleman, who had been introduced
as Colonel Mc-Somebody, engaged Larry in a
business conversation. "I want to look over
the prospectus," the man said in a raspy,
barely audible voice, "but when? Margaret

and I are leaving tomorrow morning. Making connections for that damned Mediterranean cruise she's finally talked me into. Do you have a copy of the Inter-Tex presentation with you?"

"In my room," Larry said. "You could study it on the ship and cable me if it appeals to you."

"Think it's a sound investment?" the colonel asked.

"Has D and W ever recommended one that wasn't?"

The old man considered that for a moment and then said brusquely, "Well, run up and fetch it, Delon. I'm going to have to get Margaret home before she has too many gin and tonics. And before she starts in on that midnight buffet. If she gains an ounce and can't fit into her cruise wardrobe, I'll never hear the end of it."

Larry gave Anne a look that told her this was annoying, but it was also business. The colonel was probably an old client who trusted his judgment. "I'll be right back," he promised. Anne was left in the company of the colonel.

After an awkward silence, the old man said, "Your people in the market, too?"

She really was tired. She had come close to asking "In the market for what?" Anne shook her head. "No. No, they're not."

That seemed to conclude the conversation. The old man looked around the patio, which was now becoming crowded with a motley

assortment of people. "Must find my wife," he
said. "We agreed. Just pop in and out. Pay our
respects to Millicent." Unnecessarily, he explained, "We're leaving for the mainland tomorrow morning. Tell Larry I'll be over at the
bar when he brings that prospectus down.
Fair enough?"

"Fair enough," Anne echoed.

The man shuffled off and she was left alone
in the center of a sea of strangers. She edged
toward the end of the stone floor to where the
sweeping lawn began. The air was heavy with
the scent of tropical flowers, and the shim-
mering light from the pool added an other-
worldly atmosphere to the setting. Music,
voices, smoke, intriguing aromas from the
kitchen, a caressing breeze ruffling the palm
fronds overhead. The party was unimportant;
what was thrilling was being in this far-off
paradise, a never-never land Anne had always
dreamed of visiting.

She took several steps across the velvety
lawn, then noticed that a small crushed-stone
path started up several feet away. It circled a
stone fountain that was lighted by a rose-
colored spotlight hidden in a clump of flowers.
Anne stood admiring the fountain for a few
minutes, then decided to see where the
torchlit path led.

To a carved stone bench and a flower bed,
Anne discovered. Beyond the lava-stone-
edged garden was a wall, perhaps five feet
high, formed of dark rocks. Anne guessed that
this was another, darker shade of the porous

volcanic material Larry had pointed out to her outside the airport in Honolulu. And what were those strange trees with huge leaves and clusters of green fruit growing right out of the trunks? Everything was so new and interesting and . . .

Anne gasped. She saw the dark figure catapulting over the wall before she felt the impact that sent her sprawling in the flower bed. She screamed as she fell, then lay in the softness of leaves and blossoms and newly watered soil, too stunned to move. Then someone was leaning over her. A man, breathless, his face turned away from the nearest glow of torchlight. And he was saying, "Oh, I'm sorry. I *am* sorry. Are you hurt?"

It took Anne several seconds before she could reply. Propping herself up on one elbow, she realized that the ground from which she wanted support was a mire of mud. And she could say nothing but, "Oh! Ohh! What in the world . . . ?"

The voice was deep and resonant. And very concerned. "I asked if you're hurt. Here, let me help you up."

Anne surveyed her new dress in the wavering light. The left side of it was a muddy mess. The back of it must be . . . .

"What did you think you were doing?" she cried. He had reached out for her hands, but Anne jerked aside. "I can manage, thank you!" she said sharply. Amazingly, she was none the worse for having been knocked down. She scrambled to her feet, repeating, "What did you think you were doing?"

"Taking the shortcut, as usual," the deep voice said. "Let me get you into the house and let's make sure."

"I'm not hurt," Anne insisted. "But look at me! Look at my dress!"

Whoever he was, the man must have decided that there was no need for worry. He apologized again, and then, incredibly, he started to laugh. "You'll have to redo your face after you've changed," he said.

Anne's hand went instinctively to her cheek, coming away muddy. "I'm glad you find it amusing. It happens that I don't. Leaping at people like a . . . like a maniac! You could have . . ."

"I could have hurt you, and I've already told you I'm sorry." A hand closed over Anne's forearm. "Here, let me . . ."

Anne jerked herself free. "I told you I can manage very nicely. Now, will you just . . . leap back where you came from and let me see if I can sneak into my room without . . . without making a fool of myself in front of all the guests?"

"Why do that? Most of them are so bored, you might liven things up a bit." He was laughing again. "Excuse me, but you do look . . ."

"Like something the cat dragged in?" Anne exploded. "You probably took ten years off my life! Of all the stupid brainless, idiotic—" her

angry tirade faded into a near whisper—
"dumb things to do!"

He turned and the flickering yellow light
illuminated his face. And Anne was staring at
the most unbelievably handsome man she
had ever seen. Furthermore, his coal-black
eyes were examining her face with more interest than amusement or apology. Then the
strangely disturbing gaze locked with her
own, and Anne drew a quick, involuntary
breath. They looked at each other for what
may have been several seconds or may have
been an eternity. Anne stood dumbfounded,
hearing her erratic breath, suddenly feeling
dizzy.

"It *was* a stupid thing to do," the man said.
"But the way around from driveway to driveway takes forever and I've done this before. I
listen for voices, make sure nobody's around
and . . ." He turned a devastating smile at
Anne. "It was just an impulse. I never
dreamed anyone would be anywhere but
around the pool this early in the evening.
Around the *bar* is what I really mean."

Anne searched for words. None came. She
was still angry with him for having laughed at
her. And embarrassed, imagining what she
must look like. But his explanation sounded
so sincere. And besides, she was looking up at
curling black hair that glistened under the
torchlight, at dark brows that turned up ever
so slightly at the end, giving him a built-in
expression that was part impish, part sinister.
He was tall, dressed in what appeared to be a

well-worn flowered-print shirt and faded denim shorts. Her quick glance away from his face revealed bronze and muscular legs; his shirt was unbuttoned almost to his waist, exposing a dark hairy chest and a deep tan. And he was still looking at her intently, almost insolently, as though he knew what she was seeing and was confident of her approval.

Anne felt blood rushing to her face. She started up the gravel path, more angry with herself than with the stranger. He must be thinking that his devastating good looks gave him the right to bowl people over, laugh at them, and then glory in their admiration of his physique. And she had been so obviously overwhelmed! She increased her pace, furious.

"Wait," he called out. "I'll walk you to . . ."

"Never mind!" She was running now. And evidently he had decided to go back where he had come from.

At the fountain, Anne discovered a divergence in the path that seemed to lead to the side of the house. Avoiding the patio, freezing whenever she heard a voice that sounded as though the speaker might be nearby, she made her way to a side door that took her into a solarium. No one in sight. She made several wrong turns inside the house before she reached the stairway and, finally, the sanctity of her room. A glance into the dresser mirror was depressing. Mud stains on her dress, her hands, her face. She felt like crying, taking a shower, and going to bed. But Larry would be upset if she just disappeared. And the encounter had stirred up mixed emotions that would have prevented sleep in spite of her tiredness from the long trip.

No more than fifteen minutes later, hoping no one would notice that she had changed the long muddy gown for a simple skirt and blouse, Anne eased her way back onto the crowded patio. She looked around for Larry, seeing him through the glass walls of the lanai, seated at a small well-lighted table with the old colonel and a stout overdressed woman who was probably his wife. She was feeling awkward again, wondering what to do, when a voice behind her said, "I almost didn't recognize you."

Anne turned to find herself facing the stranger she had met so unceremoniously in the garden. He was smiling, his handsome face looking devilish, amused—a trifle smug, Anne thought. "I . . . thought you'd leaped back over the wall," she said, her tone as chilly as she could make it.

"And miss another opportunity to tell you how sorry I am?" The band had started playing "The Maui Waltz" and the stranger held out his arms. "I dance much more gracefully then I leap," he said affably. "Since we're going to be neighbors, shall we declare a truce?"

Somehow, Anne was in his arms and she was being guided toward the section of the patio that had been reserved for dancing. "Neighbors?" she asked.

"I presume you're Larry's fiancée. I didn't get the name, but Millicent and the others have been talking about your arrival." The man's hold around Anne tightened. She felt uncomfortably close to his powerful body and strangely out of breath. "I'm Evan Forrester," she was told.

"Anne Beal."

"Hello, Anne." He laughed softly. "I won't say, 'We meet again.' I daresay you'd just as soon forget our first encounter."

"You . . . work next door? I didn't even know there was another house . . ."

"I live next door," Evan corrected. "I only dress like a gardener when I'm coming to one of Millicent's soirees. To demonstrate my sense of security."

Anne wasn't sure she understood that. She'd had next to nothing to drink, yet she felt giddy. Music going to her head, she guessed, and fatigue. But there was something else; something overpoweringly masculine that seemed to radiate from Evan Forrester. She felt nervous, yet the warmth of his body as he guided her through the languorously slow music was having the effect of strong wine coursing through her system. She didn't want the dance to end, yet a part of her consciousness, her *conscience*, was disturbed. She shouldn't be enjoying this moment. There was something basically wrong with feeling this tremulous, this . . . this excited.

Larry resolved her dilemma shortly afterward when he cut in, saying, "I was ready to go upstairs looking for you." He nodded to Evan, then they greeted each other casually and shook hands before Larry said, "You've changed your clothes."

"My fault," Evan said easily. He didn't explain. Maybe he would have, but Inez Carruthers appeared out of the crowd and linked her arm through his possessively. "Evan, you actually got here! I thought you were sulking because I didn't get to the harbor this morning." The attractive blonde threw a smile at Larry and then at Anne. "I couldn't get away. We had a family reunion, and Millicent doesn't take too kindly to people going sailing when a new bride is expected."

There was the faintest edge of sarcasm in Inez's tone, but perhaps Anne only imagined it. Maybe Inez was just sharing a private joke with the others: everyone seemed to know that Mrs. Delon supervised the social lives of all the people who surrounded her.

"You're forgiven," Evan said. He let himself be led off by Inez as the band started up with a thumping rock number, but not before turning to address Anne: "I hope I'm forgiven, too."

Larry didn't care much for dancing. He guided Anne toward an unoccupied table at the end of the patio, asking, "What are you supposed to forgive him for?"

Anne was forced to explain, adding, "It was . . . actually funny. I wasn't hurt, just . . . muddied up a little."

Larry saw no humor in the incident.

"Evan's not content with being the boy wonder of Hawaiian real estate. He has to play the role of irrepressible athlete, too."

"Is he . . . an old friend?" Anne asked. She couldn't disguise her curiosity about the man.

"He's not a friend," Larry said. He didn't sound curt, but he didn't sound overly pleasant either. "He bought the house and five acres next door about a year ago. Mother finds him useful as the extra unattached male at dinner parties, though they don't seem any too fond of each other. And I suspect that he's the reason Inez prolongs her visits here. The two of them share a passion for sailing." Larry shrugged. "As I suppose we all do."

Larry turned the conversation away from Evan Forrester, telling Anne that he was sorry he had neglected her, though he was certain that she would understand. Since she had been a Delon and Withrow employee, she would be a wife who could appreciate the importance of business.

Somehow, Anne had gotten through the evening without exchanging a word with her future mother-in-law. Larry saw her to her door, kissed her good night and went to his own room.

She should have been congratulating herself for having won the love of someone like Larry. The trip, this fabulous house, the knowledge that she would live in luxury for the rest of her days, should have occupied Anne's thoughts as she drifted off to sleep. But until her weariness finally took over, she could think of nothing but the thrilling sensation of a stranger's arms around her. She recalled words he had said, his sudden smile, his unbelievably handsome face, and, most of all, her own strange reaction to Evan Forrester. Not just her mind but her entire body had responded to his nearness. And when he had held her close, she had felt that it could never be close enough.

It was ridiculous and it was wrong. She was on this island to plan her wedding to Larry Delon. Every girl at the office had envied her. And yet there seemed to be no escaping the man next door.

Chapter Three

People began to fall into place the next morning. By late afternoon, Anne had all of the Delon clan sorted out in her mind. Larry was exactly as she had learned him to be; unfailingly polite, totally dependable, somewhat—she hesitated to use the word because it sounded derogatory, but it applied, nevertheless—somewhat predictable. He wanted Anne to see the island and after a sumptuous breakfast served by one of the little Filipino maids in the solarium, he drove her to Lahaina. They shopped in the quaint boutiques of what had once been a sleepy little whaling town. They had lunch in a charming, though tourist-crowded inn, and Larry found more to add to Anne's wardrobe at the Whaler's Village, a complex of new shops geared to the tourist trade. Anne was given a view of the Delons' yacht, harbored off the picturesque quay. It was a magnificent white yawl, and Anne was promised a sailing trip with Larry before he was obliged to return to Chicago.

"You didn't tell me you'd be leaving," Anne said.

Larry pressed her hand. "Somebody's got to mind the store," he told her. "You have plans to make. And you know I'll be leaving you in good hands."

Anne made her evaluations of the "good hands" later that afternoon. To begin with, there was Millicent Withrow Delon. Larry's mother, who seemed to work at dramatic entrances and exotic costumes, was unfailingly pleasant. But there was an unreal, theatrical quality about her that made Anne doubt that she would ever really know the woman. She was given to making facetious remarks, yet Anne had the feeling that beneath the sophisticated, "witty" veneer, there was a base of snobbery. Several times during the cocktail hour, and during the family dinner itself, Anne had the sensation that she was being examined with a critical eye, and that Mrs. Delon's seeming approval was a façade calculated to hide her true feelings from her elder son. At no time did Anne feel totally comfortable. She almost wished that Mrs. Delon would admit how unhappy she was that Lawrence Delon III was going to marry an unmoneyed, untraveled, naïve nobody with an undistinguished background. Instead, there were subtle reminders about the Delon name, the Delon fortune, the Delons' social distinction. If those remarks were calculated to make Anne feel out of place, they succeeded.

Warren Delon, Larry's older brother, shared his mother's snobbery, but he was apparently too pleasure-oriented to give his social position much thought. As Anne and Larry were leaving the restaurant after lunch, she could have sworn that she had seen Warren sitting at the bar, cozied up to an attractive young woman in jeans and a T-shirt. If Larry saw them, and Anne didn't know how he could help but see them, he discreetly ignored the tête-à-tête. And from the way Warren looked at Anne during the formal sit-down dinner at the Delon home, she deduced that faithfulness to his wife was not one of Warren's virtues, if, indeed, he had any at all.

Anne's negative reaction to the immediate family did not extend to Veronica Delon. The latter seemed to be resigned to her fate. Her family, Anne learned, owned one of the major knitting mills in Georgia. When it came to money and prestige, she was certainly the Delons' equal. But Veronica, either out of a reluctance to rock the boat, or because she had fallen into a comfortably lazy position and lacked the gumption to protest either her husband's drinking and philandering or her mother-in-law's well-disguised dictatorship, went along with everything in an amiable, unanimated fashion. It was only once in a while that Anne caught a touching expression in the woman's eyes—a lost look of sadness and resignation. And there was another expression that Anne caught from time to time. It was a look aimed at Anne that seemed to say, "You're about to follow in my footsteps. This is the way you manage to get along with these people."

Finally, there was Inez Carruthers. From the cocktail-hour conversation, and from comments made during dinner, Anne gathered that Inez's mother and Mrs. Delon were old school chums. Impetuous, attractive, adventurous where men were concerned, Inez was apparently more than her divorced mother could handle. She was shipped off, at least once a year, to the care of Millicent Delon, probably, Anne surmised, in the hope that the two old friends could generate a romantic interest between their respective offspring. Larry seemed no more interested in Inez than she was in him.

But Inez *did* seem to have a consuming interest. And Anne couldn't help wondering why that interest was so disturbing to her. During dinner, the animated blonde must have mentioned Evan Forrester's name more than a dozen times.

"We're going to sail around Molokai tomorrow," Inez would say.

Mrs. Delon would chortle, "How lovely, dear." And then she would say, "Perhaps Lawrence and Anne would like to join you."

Larry waved the suggestion aside. "I want to take Anne up to the Seven Sacred Pools. We're going to drive to Hana tomorrow for lunch," he added, as though that explained why he didn't want to join his mother's house guest and their neighbor.

At that point, Mrs. Delon said, almost predictably, "What a lovely idea, dear."

Didn't these people ever say what they were really thinking? Anne wondered. She felt an almost perverse need to say something totally honest. She smiled at Mrs. Delon. "It's just as well. I've never been sailing. Oh, I went out in a rowboat with my uncle Jerry . . . on this little lake in southern Illinois. But I'd probably get seasick on a real, bona fide yacht."

Warren laughed. Larry looked slightly uncomfortable. Veronica's face lighted with an amused expression, as though Anne had said and done something she herself had been longing to do. And Inez exchanged fleeting glances with her hostess, glances that said they were in the company of an alien from some other planet.

"I'm sure that if Lawrence doesn't have time to teach you to sail, we can find someone who can," Mrs. Delon said. "Evan. I'm sure we can press Evan into service."

Inez and Larry responded with looks that fell just short of being glares. Warren gulped at his dinner wine and covered up a laugh. Veronica's eyes explored the ceiling.

What strange people they were, Anne thought. You had to listen to them in two ways: once, hearing what they had said, and then once again, deciphering what they were really thinking. Maybe this was why Larry had lauded her "honesty."

But, then, Anne's outward statements were not all that honest either. Every time Evan

Forrester's name was mentioned, she felt tugged by a strong interest, a deep curiosity. She wanted the Delons to go on talking about him. Just before the cocktail hour, finding herself alone for a few minutes while Larry made a call to his secretary in Chicago, Anne had wandered out into the garden, revisiting the spot where their enigmatic neighbor had made his shortcut leap. Peering over the wall, Anne had seen that there was an adjoining tennis court, another turquoise-colored pool, another rambling glass, stone, and redwood house. Did Even live in that sprawling estate alone? It didn't seem conceivable that he wasn't married or, at least, committed to someone. How close was he to the Delons? How often did he come next door to visit?

Anne ignored her own barrage of questions. What difference did it make how often he came across that wall? And then, her curiosity intensified by a totally unjustified jealousy each time Inez mentioned the man's name, Anne had to admit to herself that, somehow, it did matter. Evan's strong aura of masculinity and power had left its indelible trace upon her consciousness, upon her body. She found herself hoping, throughout the dinner, that she would see him again—and soon. Why, for heaven's sake? She wasn't even sure that she liked the man. One thing she was sure of: she had no business feeling fluttery inside when she thought of him or heard Inez mention his name.

Given these unwelcome thoughts and confused emotions, it was a shock to Anne to hear her future mother-in-law say, during their guava sherbet dessert, that they were invited to "our dear neighbor's little hovel" for a party that evening. "I think it's a matter of guilt," Mrs. Delon said in her usual facetious manner. "Evan's been here to a half dozen parties the past month or two. He's not terribly social, but I expect that if he gives one huge bash he'll figure that he's paid back all his obligations."

"Do we have to go?" Larry asked.

Anne felt her breath suspended in her lungs until Mrs. Delon said, "We've got to make an appearance, darling. I should think you'd want to. The dear boy might want to diversify. After all, Hawaiian real estate does have its limitations."

Was it for business reasons that Larry decided that, yes, they should all stroll over to Evan Forrester's party? It didn't matter to Anne why she was going. She only knew that she took an inordinate amount of time getting dressed, choosing the butterfly-printed teal-blue silk sarong Larry had insisted upon buying for her earlier in the day, and rearranging her hair three times before she was satisfied with the result. Even Larry commented on her eye makeup when they met in the patio at eight thirty. "You're becoming a bit of a glamour girl," he said. Anne thanked him for the compliment and walked over to the house next door with her hand clasped in that of her husband-to-be. But her nervous sense of anticipation had nothing to do with Larry.

Few of the guests who had attended the Delons' party the night before were present at Evan Forrester's affair. For one thing, there were quite a number of Hawaiian locals. There were no retired military types. And Anne felt almost conspicuously overdressed in her new silk sarong. This was a young, informally dressed crowd and everyone seemed perfectly at ease. Only Inez, who arrived in tight white jeans and a pink-and-white-striped tank top, seemed to know what was expected.

Anne had consumed two cocktails and danced one dance with Larry and another with his brother, shrinking under Warren's clammy and too personal touch, before their host freed himself from a large crowd of guests and made his way toward them.

Anne had arrived determined to put her feelings about Evan Forrester into perspective. Her reaction to his sudden presence was purely involuntary. He was dressed in white ducks, a yachting cap perched jauntily on his dark, curling hair. And, this time, the sexuality that he exuded was almost a palpable force. Yet he was gracious to Larry, made light banter with Mrs. Delon, unhooked Inez's arm when she made one of her possessive moves. His dark eyes examined Anne as though he were taking inventory in a warehouse, a look that she resented but which left her suddenly weak.

It was not long before Evan separated himself from his other guests, and Larry became engrossed in a conversation with a sunbronzed widow who was visiting Maui as part of a round-the-world sailing trip and had dogmatic opinions about "hard investments" versus "soft investments," whatever that might mean. Anne found herself being escorted on a tour of the gardens, her host behaving one minute as though she was no more interesting to him than the tropical vegetation and the next minute as though he had a right to his proprietary air, linking his arm through Anne's, guiding her through the maze of paths by placing an arm around her waist, acting as though he owned her! And how confusing it was to pretend that she felt no reaction to the touch of his hand, that she did not resent or welcome the accidental brushes of his hands that were not, Anne felt, totally accidental!

"There, you see?" They had come to a garden spot where the stone wall dipped, following the curve of the gently sloping terrain. "Can you see how tempting it would be to hop over at this spot, instead of going all the way up the driveway to the gate and then repeating the process from the Delons' entryway? One well-timed leap and I'm there."

"And your neighbor's house guest is in the flower bed," Anne reminded him.

Evan gestured at the stone bench and waited until Anne had seated herself before he said, "From what I've seen of the Delons' house guests, a muddy flower bed is an ideal place for them." He sat down. "Present company excepted, of course. And Inez, too. She looks better hoisting sails."

Evan dropped down, sitting closer to Anne than she felt he needed to. His arm, his leg, even through the fabric that separated them, felt disturbingly warm and muscular against her own. Covering up her sudden nervousness, Anne said, "You don't sound overly fond of your neighbors' friends."

"Or my neighbors," Evan said carelessly.

Anne was shocked by his bluntness. "That's a . . . strange thing to say. You seem willing enough to accept their hospitality."

"As I said, on occasion the Delons have visitors who are worth meeting." His short laugh sounded malicious to Anne. "Currently, they have two."

"And this one happens to be engaged to Larry Delon," Anne reminded him. She sounded almost prim and she was afraid that Evan would laugh at her. She moved away from him, trying to sound less stuffy now. "After the middle of June, you'll be including me in your . . . rude evaluation of the family."

"And that's going to be a pity," Evan conceded. His dark eyes met Anne's, but only for an instant; she had to turn away from the penetrating stare. "You're really serious about going through with this . . . marriage?"

He had placed such a scathing inflection on the word "marriage" that Anne's mild annoyance turned to anger. "What kind of question is that supposed to be?"

"An honest one." He was infuriatingly calm. "It just occurred to me, having met good old Millicent, and that lush who will soon be your brother-in-law, and his poor little wife."

Anne stood abruptly. "How can you possibly talk that way about people whose hospitality you've accepted? People who happen to be your guests right now!"

Evan got to his feet. "There's quite a difference between having a few drinks with people who happen to live next door to you and spending the rest of your life with them. From what I've heard about you . . ."

"What can you possibly have heard about me?" Anne flared. "You don't know the first thing . . ."

"And you underestimate my ear for snide innuendos," Evan cut in. "Of course the family's discussed you. At great length."

"I don't like inferences," Anne said. "If you're implying that . . . that they don't approve of me . . ."

"They barely approve of each other," Evan said. "You didn't think they'd fall all over themselves over . . . one of Lawrence's employees?"

Something inside her told Anne that Evan was imitating Mrs. Delon's voice as he said "employees." It was as though the word was meant to be belittling, almost insulting. Was he inventing the alleged discussion? Even if he had heard derogatory remarks about Anne, how could he be so callous as to repeat them? Even worse, hint at them, leaving the rest to Anne's imagination? She felt a sudden distaste for the Delon family, but even more for this insufferable stranger. She felt her cheeks burning and wanted only to escape from this conversation. But she was determined to save face. "Larry and I don't much care what other people think," she said. "And I'm marrying him, not his family."

Evan made a derisive sound. "Ask Veronica about that."

"I don't have to consult with anybody. I'm not Veronica."

"Precisely why I'm wondering what would make you step into this gilded trap," Evan said.

"Do you always meddle in other people's business?" Anne demanded. "Did it ever occur to you that two people can . . . two people can be . . . ?"

She cursed herself for being unable to complete the sentence. She had wanted to say something about two people being very much in love. But the coal-black eyes were exploring hers with a smug, knowing expression, as though Evan were reading her mind. He was carrying his cocktail glass, as was Anne. Now he raised it slightly and said, "Shall we drink to true love?" A sardonic half-smile crossed

his handsome features. "Or to solid investments?"

It took Anne several seconds to understand
what was meant by the sarcastic question.
The man's nerve was beyond belief! "That's
the most insulting, presumptuous . . ."

"And irritatingly honest observation you've
ever heard," Evan said. He took a slow sip
from his drink. "It does sound a little trite,
doesn't it? I've jumped at such an obvious
conclusion. Girl from unmoneyed background
is suddenly given the opportunity to marry the
scion of a wealthy, socially prominent family.
One usually sees it only in those very bad
movies they show on late-night television, but
when it does actually happen, I imagine it
must be hard to resist. All those seasons in
Switzerland and cruises to Nassau."

"You're being absolutely vile!" Anne cried
out. "Implying that I'd marry someone for his
money . . . why, that makes me just a cut
above being a . . . a . . . prostitute!"

"Your word, not mine," Evan said. He
placed his almost empty glass on the stone
bench. Then, methodically, although her
glass was more than half full, he took Anne's
drink out of her hand and placed it beside his.
Before Anne could recover from the puzzling
gesture, she felt Evan's hands close over her
shoulders. "If I'm wrong, then you must be
the most inexperienced, naïve, blind creature
on God's green earth."

A shiver ran through her at the touch of his

hands. But Anne forced herself to remain cool, to sound aloof and self-possessed. "I've never claimed to be 'experienced,' Mr. Forrester. I don't think I'm naïve. And I certainly . . ."

She hadn't run out of words this time. Anne's sentence was stopped abruptly by a swift motion. Evan's hands pulled her forward, then dropped from her shoulders. In the next instant, his arms had closed around her in a steely grip, pulling her hard against his chest. She let out a small cry of protest, but this, too, was lost as Evan's mouth closed over hers, pressing it in a fierce, exploratory kiss. She struggled for a moment to free herself, then realized that he was too strong. All she could do was submit to the bruising pressure against her mouth, then the demanding, unrelenting exploration that made her feel as though she was being possessed. Her only retaliation was to remain passive, to pretend indifference if not resistance. She would show him that she not only did not respond to his unwelcome embrace but that she . . . that she . . .

That she what? Found the heat of his lips against hers repulsive? He was awakening in her a passion she did not know existed! She tried to hold herself rigid, but as Evan's hands caressed her back, she felt herself melting, her entire body letting go, fusing against the firm, muscular chest, her lips responding, her entire physical being wanting him closer.

He let Anne go as abruptly as he had seized

her. And, as breathless as she was, he was gazing at her now with a pleased, challenging expression, telling her silently that she had liked what he had done, that she would welcome an even closer contact with him.

Fury with him, and with herself, raced like a searing fire through Anne's nerves. She tried to say something scathing. She thought of slapping him, but that would have been too melodramatic and would probably have been a boon to his already inflated ego. She wanted to scream or to cry or to run, but confusion froze her on the spot. And the only words that finally came to her were a weak, half-whispered question: "Why did you do that?"

Evan turned to pick up the two glasses from the bench. "For the same reason I leaped over the wall, Anne. Because it occurred to me."

"And you follow every instinct like a . . . like a . . ."

"Like an honest animal," Evan said, handing Anne her drink. She ignored him and he held both glasses in his hands and added, "No, that wasn't the only reason. If I don't accept the fact that you're marrying Lawrence Delon the Third for his money, then I've got to believe that you really haven't known many men. I honestly do think you ought to broaden your experience before you make a major commitment that you might live to regret."

"And you're just smug enough to think that you're so marvelous by comparison that . . ."

"That you might realize something very

important: all kisses are not as matter-of-fact as a meeting of stockholders with the chairman of the board."

His conceit was beyond belief. Anne felt a rushing need to stand up for the man she was going to marry, to let this egotistical creature know that Larry was romantic, Larry's kisses excited her, Larry promised a wedding night that would fulfill all her most romantic daydreams. But she decided that Larry didn't need defending, certainly not before this insolent boor. "If you'll excuse me," she said, "I'd like to join my fiancé and ask him to take me home."

She sounded so priggish that she was embarrassed, especially since Evan only smiled at her faintly, his expression revealing that he was now even more pleased with himself than before. After which he said, in a tone he might have used to comment on the weather, "I'd wait until I got my lipstick unsmeared if I were you. And until I caught my breath."

"Ohh!" There were no words to describe him. Anne turned on her heels and started a purposeful march down the path toward the patio, her insides churning.

She was close to the sound of voices when she realized two things simultaneously. One, Evan was not dashing after her, but letting her go ahead alone just as he had done the evening before. And two, his practical advice had been sound. Her mouth felt bruised; it felt almost as though Evan's kiss was burned there for everyone to see. She was sure that her lipstick was a mess and that everyone at the party, and Larry in particular, would notice that immediately. She had left her small handbag on one of the tables near the pool. What could she do to erase the visible effect of Evan Forrester's unwanted attention?

But there was more than the visible effect to be repaired. Evan had taken some perverse delight in pointing out to her the emotional impact of his prolonged kiss. She was panting like a long-distance runner at the end of a grueling race.

Tonight there was no possibility of sneaking around to the side of the house and later making a discreet re-entrance. Anne licked her lips, hoping the smears would not be too obvious. She stopped to draw a deep breath, releasing it slowly and then repeating the exercise. She lifted her chin, braced her shoulders, and walked as casually as she was able. By the time she reached the patio area, she imagined herself to be totally under control.

As had happened the night before, the party seemed to have drawn together a motley crowd. People stood around in groups of three or more. A few were dancing to a currently popular ballad, but most were crowded around the bamboo bar. Anne looked around for Larry, then for some other familiar face. She was on her way toward the sliding glass doors that led to Evan's living room, thinking she might find Larry there, when she brushed past a trio of people standing next to a lava-stone waterfall. She hadn't glanced at their faces, but as she moved toward the house she heard a shrill and chillingly recognizable voice.

"Anne! Oh, my dear, you haven't fallen off the world after all! Lawrence has been looking everywhere for you!"

Anne turned to see Mrs. Delon, a martini glass in one of her ring-laden hands, dramatic in her long hand-embroidered white cotton tent dress. "Oh . . . oh, I'm sorry, Mrs. Delon. I just . . ." Once again, words eluded her and her face felt flushed.

Fortunately, Larry's mother rarely waited for replies or explanations. "You do have a way of disappearing," the older woman said in an airy tone. She waved at two rather dissipated middle-aged people. "Charles, Beryl— do meet Lawrence's lovely little friend from the mainland. Anne, these are my very dear friends, Dr. and Mrs. Temple."

Anne had a dim impression of acknowledgments, then of some inane chit-chat about Chicago, where the doctor had served one year of his residency. And then Larry joined them, placing a protective arm around Anne and telling her that he had been just about to go back to their own house to check on her. Was she sure that she was all right?

"Of course she is," Mrs. Delon said firmly. "She's just gone for a little stroll and . . . oh, dear, she seems to have lost our host somewhere in the coconut grove. We can't very well leave without saying good night to Evan, but, frankly, I never intended to stay any longer than to pay my respects. Lawrence, shall we round up the rest, or do you propose to stay on?"

It was all rattled off in Mrs. Delon's seemingly facetious manner, an affectation that was as typical of her as the exotic dresses and jewelry she wore. But she had also managed to let Larry know that Anne had been in the garden with Evan Forrester.

Happily, Larry was too stolid and too secure to make anything of that. He tightened his hold around Anne, which had now shifted to her waist. It was as if he hadn't heard his mother, or, if he had, thought nothing of Anne's being shown around the grounds by their host. "If you're ready to leave," he said, "I'll gather up the clan."

Mrs. Delon had said that the others might want to stay, yet, it seemed to Anne, when Larry's mother decided it was time to leave, it was time for everyone in the family to follow suit.

Larry excused himself and went in search of the other three members of their party, jokingly telling Anne, "Stay right here, dear. I don't want to lose you again."

"I doubt that you will," Mrs. Delon said. This time her voice was not shrill. She almost purred the words. And at the same time, unseen by Larry as he started toward the bar, Millicent Withrow Delon fixed Anne with a strange little smile. If there was disapproval in her expression, it was extremely subtle.

And, later, after Larry had kissed her good night at her bedroom door, a kiss that left her unmoved, Anne had time to remember Mrs. Delon's look and to analyze it. No, it hadn't been critical. But it had been *knowing*, Anne thought. And, incredibly, Anne had seen in the narrowed, pale blue eyes, a look of . . . no, that would have made no sense. But the impression persisted. It had been a look of smug satisfaction.

Guilt-ridden, Anne checked her face in the bathroom mirror. Her lipstick was not smudged; it was nonexistent. Had Mrs. Delon noticed Anne's carefully made-up mouth while they were all walking to Evan's place?

For a short while, as she changed into her nightgown, Anne pondered the enigmatic expression. But Mrs. Delon did not occupy her thought for long. There was another disturbing moment to remember, a moment during which a thoroughly detestable, egocentric, snide man had held her in his arms, held her so closely that the maleness of him was like molten metal in her veins. She should have fought him off like a wildcat, slapped his face afterward and run from him. But she had let herself be swept into the fervor of his kiss. She had let her body fuse against his as though this was a wanted intimacy, a passion they both shared. And he had only been testing her, showing off his masculine superiority, making a complete and utter fool of her to prove his point. Anne flopped on the bed, furious.

Her fist pounded against the pillow in frustration. She wanted to cry, but there were no tears inside her. Just the burning knowledge that she had let a detestable man insult her, insult Larry, and then ridicule her because he had left her breathless. What had Mrs. Delon seen in her face? Anne didn't know. But one thing she *did* know. She never wanted to see Evan Forrester again.

Chapter Four

$\mathscr{L}$ arry made a determined effort to show Anne as much of Maui as possible before it was necessary for him to return to pressing business in Chicago. During drives along the twisting road to Hana, where they had discovered a crystal-clear pool at the foot of a splashing waterfall that made an idyllic picnic spot, or listening to Hawaiian music at one of the swank new hotels, Anne found herself once again thinking that she was extremely fortunate. Larry was unfailingly thoughtful and kind.

There were several more parties at the homes or condominiums of family friends. If she was never introduced to the Delons' usually middle-aged friends as Larry's future wife, Anne was untroubled, nor did she feel slighted. There was a reason for this, she discovered. The invitation list for her wedding was apparently not going to be the same as Mrs. Delon's casual lists for cocktails or dinner. It was Veronica who said, "Millicent enjoys mixing all sorts of people at these little functions. Sort of a . . . madcap, fun thing.

But a wedding is something else. *Those* people will be carefully screened, believe me."

Anne didn't ask on what basis the wedding guests would be "screened." She wouldn't be discussing wedding plans with Larry's mother until he was back at his desk. Meanwhile, he monopolized all her time and filled the week with exploring the island and socializing. She reveled in the beauty of Maui, in the balmy weather, the luxury of being waited on by the always obliging servants.

She saw very little of Larry's brother and sister-in-law. Veronica seemed to have a few friends of her own on the island and was busy learning a small part in a play the local theater group would be presenting in another month. Warren either lounged around the pool area with a drink in his hand or sped off in one of the sports cars to some unnamed destination. They seemed to go their separate ways.

Mrs. Delon kept busy with luncheon dates, her hairdresser—an almost daily ritual—and with entertaining and being entertained by people who were apparently not going to be invited to her son's forthcoming marriage. If the conversations among the family members sometimes seemed shallow and unreal, they were also undisturbing. The interviews Anne had dreaded never materialized; there were no references to the difference between Anne's background and Larry's. Anne decided that Evan Forrester's implication that Anne had been discussed by the Delons in uncomplimentary terms was a figment of his imagination. Like his sudden display of machismo and his disdain for the Delon family, the snide suggestion that Anne was something less than welcome was just one more proof that he was a decidedly unlikable person.

Yet there were at least two parties during which Anne found herself looking through the crowd as though expecting that Evan might be there. She assured herself that she had no desire to see him; if anything, she wanted to know if he was present so that she could avoid him. Neither time did Evan make an appearance.

On one occasion, gathering flowers from which Guadalupe and Amalia had promised to teach Anne the art of making woven leis, Anne had lingered in the garden to listen to symphonic music pouring forth from the house next door. She had filled her basket with palapalai ferns and plumeria blossoms; there was no reason for her to stand near the stone wall, her basket resting on the stone bench where Evan had placed their drinks before he clasped her in his arms. Yet, there was something that held her there. Was Evan at home, listening to the stirring, dramatic music? Was he alone?

Anne had torn herself away from the spot in sudden anger with herself. What difference did it make? And what if he had seen her there, looking toward his house? What if he had noticed her listening, standing there as though she hoped to get a glimpse of him,

as though she half hoped he would come
bounding over the wall? His already inflated
ego would soar! He would feel more smug
than ever! Anne almost ran back to the
house.

It was late in the week before Anne actually
saw him, and then only briefly. She was on
her way to the driveway, where Larry was
waiting for her. He was leaving the next day
and had asked Anne to help him select some
"token remembrances" for the office staff.
Anne had run back to her room for her sunglasses. She was barely out of the house
before she saw Evan approaching. Involuntarily, she caught her breath. She made a
concentrated effort to look as though she were
in a hurry and couldn't care less about the
unexpected visit of a neighbor.

How irritating it was to have him so aware
of her emotional reaction to him, her every
effort to cover it up! Evan smiled knowingly
as though he had seen her suck in that quick
breath of air and was now seeing that she was
deliberately pretending indifference to the
sight of him.

"Aloha," he said. His smile, contrasted
with his sun-bronzed skin, was devastating.
He wore tennis whites and sneakers, but a
navy blue yachting cap, sitting at a jaunty
angle, covered most of his gleaming black
hair. He must know how fantastic he
looks, Anne thought. He must enjoy his effect upon stupid, romantically inclined fe-
males.

She responded with a mechanical, "Aloha, yourself," and started to hurry on.

"You're in a terrible rush," Evan commented. "You'll have to get used to island time."

Anne hesitated, "Oh?"

"Meaning, you'll get there whenever you're darned good and ready."

"I don't think Larry would appreciate that this morning," Anne said stiffly. "We have some last-minute shopping to do."

Evan seemed surprised. "You're leaving?"

"*He's* leaving," Anne said. "But he'll be back, of course."

"Of course. But in the meantime, we'll have to get together."

"I don't think you understand," Anne told him. "I'm engaged to be married. I'm not free to . . ."

"I was going to ask if you'd like to go sailing." Evan looked at her as though she were behaving like a prim old spinster. "Sailing. Everybody here does it. I didn't ask you to go to bed with me."

Anne gasped. He had a talent for humiliating her. She mumbled something about being busy with wedding plans. "I doubt that I'll have time."

"If I know old Millicent, she'll do your planning for you," Evan said. "You play tennis, I presume?"

"I never had time to learn," Anne snapped. She was tired of being reminded that she didn't belong with this leisure class, fun-and-

68

games set. "I'm the poor working girl, remember? The one who's marrying a terrible old man for his money."

Evan laughed and Anne felt better. "Score one point for Cinderella," he said. "But keep in mind that tennis is teachable. So is sailing. I have dozens of talented protégés to prove it."

"I'll bet," Anne said under her breath.

He seemed to find that amusing, too. "But, be assured that I don't kiss all of them. I've been teaching a wonderful sixty-three-year-old lady to sail. And learning a few pointers myself from a crazy blonde who was supposed to have met me out front. Is Inez around?"

"I haven't seen her," Anne said. Why this sudden sinking feeling? Had she thought Evan was making a morning call to see *her*?

"Probably still asleep," Evan said. But he did not move aside yet; it seemed that he was blocking Anne's way deliberately. "We were out dancing until two."

Somehow, that statement was even more disturbing. Why should she care? Evan and Inez were ideally suited to each other. Neither seemed to do anything productive. Both seemed to live only for pleasure. She couldn't resist making a snippy comment of her own. "Don't you ever work?"

"At least four hours a day," Evan replied easily. He tapped his forehead. "Up here. Sign of a well-organized executive. I sit down, listen to Beethoven, make a few phone calls. And I manage to keep a lot of people employed." Out of the blue, he asked, "Do you like Beethoven?"

Was she going to have to tell him that most of the people in her small town knew nothing but country and western music? "That's another area I've never had a chance to explore." With all the sarcasm she could muster, she added, "Make a note, Mr. Forrester. I've never gone to a grand opening at the opera, either. But when I was five, I could play 'Turkey in the Straw' on a comb."

Oddly, he didn't think that was funny. Anne looked up to see that his usually cynical expression had softened. "But I know you like beautiful music." He reached out to place his fingers against Anne's face. It was a gentle touch, totally unexpected, and it reduced Anne to breathlessness once again. And although the soft caress of his fingers had no sexual overtones, she felt a sharp quickening inside herself, an overpowering awareness of his virility.

There were two short toots of an automobile horn from the driveway. "I . . . I've really got to run," Anne said. She didn't know what made her ask the question that followed. Evan's hand was still touching her face and she spoke in a quavering tone. "How . . . how did you know I like beautiful music?"

He withdrew his fingers. And now he was Evan Forrester again, sardonic, aware of his effect upon women, taking enjoyment out of reminding them that he was irresistible. "My study's on the third level. A little aerie where I can be alone when I work. You can't see it from the garden here, but I can peer through those tall coco palms and see the spot where we met."

Uncomfortable, Anne started to move around him. "I don't know what you're talking about."

"I'm only answering your quesion. I watched you the other day. Lovely lady with a basket of ferns and flowers, looking very beautiful, but . . . a little wistful, I thought. And staring for the longest time toward . . . the house where I live."

"You flatter yourself," she said. Anne made a quick move to walk around him. "Maybe you mistook someone else for me."

She was hurrying around the house toward the driveway when she heard Evan call out, "No. I know one Delon house guest from the other."

Anne didn't turn back, but she spoke loudly enough so that he couldn't help hearing her. "That's easy. Inez is the one who sleeps late and I'm the one who's getting married in June. There shouldn't be any confusion in your mind."

Evan's laughter followed her almost all the way to the spot where Larry sat behind the wheel of the white Porsche waiting for her.

"Something wrong?" Larry asked when she had gotten into the little sports car beside him. "I thought you were just going to run up to your room for your sunglasses."

"I did," Anne said. "I . . . I'd misplaced them."

She lied badly. Had Larry seen Evan coming up the walk? He must have. To cover up for her senseless trembling, Anne decided to tell him the truth. "And then your neighbor . . . what's his name . . . Evan came up looking for Inez. I had to explain to him that we didn't see her at breakfast and so forth and so on."

Larry was gunning the car toward the entry gates. "What's . . . 'so forth and so on'?"

"Oh, you know . . . the usual small talk." Larry sounded, for the first time since she had promised to marry him, as though he might be jealous. Had he gotten out of the car, tired of waiting for her, walked toward the house and seen Evan touching her face? Why had she let him do that?

Well, there was no point in spoiling this fun day of shopping by allowing that arrogant person to embarrass her and then make her feel guilty! She couldn't think of anything more to say. At least nothing that wouldn't sound as though she were being purposefully casual and covering up her tension, so she might as well let it drop.

Fortunately, Larry did not pursue the matter. They drove to a charming shopping complex geared for tourists and spent several hours selecting gifts for employees at Delon and Withrow and for Larry's friends in Chicago. It should have been a lark, but there was something businesslike and methodical about

Larry's selections. "We don't want anything that looks like a cheap souvenir," he said, "but we don't want anything ostentatious either. Both extremes would be in bad taste." Anne felt self-conscious about making suggestions; how could she be certain that her taste was as good as Larry's?

Several times, during lunch in a glassed-in seafood restaurant that overlooked the sea, Anne's thoughts wandered back to her meeting, that morning, with Evan Forrester. How could he be so charming one moment and so detestable the next? And why had she let him seep into her consciousness, so that his words rang in her ears while Larry was trying to have a conversation with her? She was going to have to make a deliberate attempt to forget that Evan existed. With Larry gone, it was going to be especially important that she avoid the man who stirred such disturbingly mixed emotions inside her.

It was upsetting, too, to sit at the dinner table with the Delon family that evening and to hear them discussing trips and activities and people with which, and to whom, Anne could not relate. Would she always feel like an outsider among these people?

"I'll be gone about three weeks," Larry explained as dessert was served. "I know you will all do your best to keep Anne busy and happy."

"Don't worry about your little Anne," said Mrs. Delon smoothly. "I have all sorts of plans for her. You may not even know her when you get back!"

Anne could not help noticing that Mrs. Delon's smile was cold and politely social. She had the feeling that her future mother-in-law could hardly wait for Larry's departure to start molding Anne closer to the image that she had in mind—the sort of wife she wanted for her son. To Anne's ears even Larry's protests that he liked her just the way she was sounded more dutiful than sincere.

Later that night, when the others had drifted off to a party aboard the yacht of some newly arrived friends, Larry took Anne out to the dimly lighted lanai. He folded her in his arms and kissed her repeatedly, murmuring words of love. Anne tried to respond.

"I love you, I love you," she assured him in answer to his repeated question, as much to convince herself as to convince Larry.

"Tell me, darling, that you'll miss me," he whispered in her ear.

But even as she whispered the tender words that he begged for, she heard the passionate strains of music pouring out from the house next door. Unbidden, another face rose to haunt her—a face with penetrating dark eyes that looked deeply into her own.

No! It was all a lie! Terrible, incredible, frightening as it was—she wouldn't miss Larry at all. Not at all.

Chapter Five

$\mathcal{M}$rs. Delon barely waited until Larry was on the plane before she began her campaign. There were subtle hints about Anne's clothing, her need to acquaint herself with "Lawrence's life-style," her tendency to reveal too much about her humble origins to total strangers. Anne would have reacted sharply if the hints had not been so delicately phrased; one could never be certain that Millicent Delon was being serious.

Then, when a planning session for the wedding was called, Anne began to have her first touch of queasiness about the entire affair. Apparently, it was going to be an extravaganza. Mrs. Delon had jotted down hundreds of names; people would be flying to Maui from all parts of the world, and they were the social elite. The ceremony itself would be conducted by a distinguished minister, an old family friend who would be flown to the island from Boston. Mrs. Delon had every detail worked out, from the caterers to the clothing to be worn by the bridal party. Nor did she ask Anne's opinion about any of the arrangements. Veronica sat during the meeting, which was more like a monologue, adding nothing to the plans, only nodding vaguely when Mrs. Delon said, "I know you must be thinking that planning is the bride's prerogative, my dear, but you do understand that our family has a great social responsibility to old friends and to our clients. Since you can't possibly know . . . since you haven't had the experience . . . I do hope you will let me relieve you of the burden." She didn't wait for Anne's response. "We'll trust LeCaille with the gowns for you and the bridesmaids, of course. He did the most magnificent designs when Warren and Veronica were married. Really, Anne, all you have to worry about is letting me know if there is someone very close you might want as an attendant so that we can arrange for fittings. LaCaille is quartered in New York, but he will fly anywhere if the occasion is important enough. You'll want to give me your list. And, of course, I know you will be as selective as we are being."

"I'll go to work on it," Anne said. She felt depressed and resentful. Her selective list would consist of her father, who would feel hopelessly out of place in this milieu, and a few school and office friends who could afford neither the time nor the money to travel to Hawaii for a wedding. Was it too late to talk with Larry and change his mother's plan for a major social event? A simple wedding in Chicago, affordable by the bride's family—would that be asking too much? She could merely glance at Mrs. Delon and know that such a suggestion would be unthinkable. How could she have let this most important day in her life get so completely out of her control?

She couldn't muster up the nerve to complain to Larry when he phoned her early that evening. She heard herself repeating his words, sounding mechanical: "I love *you*." It was an effort to think of herself as the lucky girl who was the envy of all her co-workers at Delon and Withrow.

Without Larry to squire her around, Anne found the days that followed long and empty. She watched Evan and Inez leaving the house on two consecutive mornings and knew that Inez did not return until late at night. Why the tug of jealousy when the two of them went off to spend the day on Evan's yacht? She was avoiding him with good reason, wasn't she? Why this nervous restlessness?

Mrs. Delon must have sensed that Anne was not enjoying herself. At breakfast one morning, she announced that she'd had "an absolutely brilliant inspiration." Anne certainly wanted to adapt herself to the activities that were important in Lawrence's life. Certainly she would want to learn to sail. The Delon's yacht, the *Deedubble-U*, was too large for teaching purposes, but their next-door neighbor, in addition to his sixty-two-foot motor sailer, owned a small sloop that would

be exactly right for a total beginner. "And I'm
sure he could be pressed into service," Mrs.
Delon went on. "Don't you think so, Inez?"

If Inez disapproved of the idea, she was
clever enough to disguise the fact. "Oh, he
loves turning people on to sailing. We've been
going almost every morning. Why don't you
join us one of these days, Anne?"

That, apparently, was not what Mrs. Delon
had in mind. "You'd be too inhibiting, darling.
I certainly wouldn't want a three-time Maui-
to-Honolulu-Regatta winner around if *I* were
a total neophyte. I'll have Evan make the
arrangements."

No one asked Anne what she thought of the
idea. And later, when she confided in Veronica that she wasn't too sure Larry would approve, Veronica said in her quiet, resigned
tone, "Oh, I'm sure Larry wouldn't object.
Evan certainly isn't a threat. He's the peren-
nial bachelor! So far he has managed to avoid
romantic entanglements with dozens of
wealthy and attractive young women while
teaching them his favorite sport. He certainly hasn't given Inez any encouragement.
Heaven knows she's done everything she can
to invite it!"

Though Veronica was too polite to say it, the
implication was clear. Evan Forrester was
pursued by so many women it was unlikely
that he would be interested in a mere office
worker from a small coal-mining town in
Illinois.

"I'm afraid he'll resent being stuck with

me," Anne said. "I hope Mrs. Delon forgets about *that* plan."

Veronica looked around, as if to make sure she would not be overheard. "Anne, believe me, she never forgets about an idea once it's occurred to her. It occurred to her once that Warren should settle down with a wife. It also occurred to her that I would be a suitable candidate." Veronica smiled, but there was a sadness about her eyes. "And . . . here I am!"

Anne couldn't help liking Veronica, but she found it hard to respect her. Surely she knew that her husband was a weak, tipsy philanderer. And surely she must have had some plans for her own life. Yet she seemed content to let Mrs. Delon make all the major decisions for her, placidly going along with her mother-in-law's every whim, as though her own character were made of putty. "I won't let that happen to me," Anne told herself. Yet she *was* letting it happen. Why? Because she was insanely in love with Larry and would do anything to keep him?

No. It was because it would all be different after they were married, Anne told herself. They would live away from his family, in Chicago. Larry was too strong, and he loved Anne too much, to let his mother duplicate her velvet-gloved mastery over Warren and Veronica.

It wasn't until she was alone in her room that night that Anne began to think of the possibility that she would be spending time alone with Evan Forrester. She had made no objection to Mrs. Delon's idea that Evan might be called upon to teach Anne one of the family "musts." It would be embarrassing to have him around under those circumstances. Yet, he had already made the suggestion himself. Maybe he would find some pretext on which to refuse. Anne had certainly let him know that she wasn't interested. Or had she? Had she really?

Two days went by. Inez Carruthers appeared to absorb Evan's time. One morning Anne decided to go to the beach. It was the only way, she decided, to escape Mrs. Delon's plan-of-the-day, to teach her bridge. She was just getting into the white sports car when Evan strolled into the garden.

Anne had thrown a short white terrycloth coverup over her bikini. With little to do since Larry's departure, she had spent hours lolling around the pool and had acquired a honey-gold tan. She was acutely conscious of Evan's eyes on her. She felt as though her entire body was exposed and experienced the same fluttery feeling that always accompanied Evan's nearness.

"Running away from the dragon?" he mocked her.

"Just to the beach," Anne told him. She tossed her straw tote bag onto the car seat.

"Alone?" Evan leaned against the car, lifting an eyebrow in speculation.

"Of course, alone." Anne made an attempt to look as though she were in a hurry. She

avoided looking at Evan, though she had noticed that he was wearing dark swimming
trunks and a Hawaiian print shirt that was
opened to reveal his deeply tanned muscular
chest. Even the quick glance at him had made
a disturbing physical impact on her. "I just
. . . wanted to get away for a while."

"By yourself," Evan said. "That's an amaz-
ing coincidence. I was thinking of going somewhere to be alone myself. Why don't we do it
together? Being alone is always more interesting when you have someone to share it with."

She wanted to say something sprightly and
careless in return, but she felt tongue-tied.
Just the thought that Evan wanted to be with
her left her weak with excitement. And she
couldn't help wondering if someone in the
house was watching.

Could Evan read her mind? "If you're concerned about being seen with me, please
relax. Her Nibs has already suggested that I
might be useful as an instructor. In other
words, I've been approved."

"I assume you're referring to Mrs. Delon,"
Anne said in what she hoped was a haughty
tone.

"I am. As delicately as possible, I let her
know that I didn't make command performances. That if I felt like teaching you to sail
or to play tennis, I'd do it of my own volition
. . . not because she wanted me to. Independence, Annie. Never lose your independence."

Anne liked his attitude. She needed to be

bolstered, needed to let Mrs. Delon know that she was no Veronica. Just deciding to skip the bridge lesson and go to the beach had been a big step. Going to the beach with Evan would be another. She got into the car, seated herself behind the wheel and smiled. "I'd probably get lost by myself," she said. "Come along, if you want to."

"You'll share your towel with me?" Evan had started to circle the car, then stopped. "If not, we can stop at my place."

"I'll share my towel with you," Anne said. She felt suddenly capricious and young. Yes, and more than that. She felt suddenly *free*. She hadn't realized how oppressive it was to be around people who wanted you to be something you weren't.

It was even a minor satisfaction to see Inez walking out into the patio, her customary morning bloody mary in hand. She would be watching as the car purred out of the driveway. It was a petty satisfaction, Anne realized, but as she drove toward the gates with Evan in the seat beside her, her heart was beating a fast, pleasurable tattoo.

It was a glorious sun-drenched day, with just enough of a fresh breeze from the ocean to ruffle Anne's hair and add to her sense of freedom. As she drove along the curving highway, there were occasional glimpses of the ocean, a changing turquoise green capped with lacy white froth. She managed quick glimpses of Evan, too. His dark curling hair shone in the bright light. His profile was strong and perfectly delineated. He was so handsome that he looked unreal, Anne thought. She had no business feeling this exhilarated by his closeness! She was an about-to-be-married, sensible young woman, in love with a wonderful man who loved her in return. She would have to keep reminding herself that this was a meaningless lark. She must not lose sight of the fact that Evan enjoyed pursuing and being pursued. She would enjoy this time with him, Anne promised herself. But she would keep it in perspective. A day at the beach with a neighbor. Nothing more.

Evan didn't leave her time for introspection. He pointed out a turnoff that led to a long white stretch of sandy beach. Anne pulled up under a stand of twisted evergreen trees. The beach was completely deserted. One battered picnic table, a portable dressing room, and an outdoor shower were the only refinements. A few swaying palm trees dotted the palisades.

"Beautiful!" Anne said aloud. She grabbed her straw bag and got out of the car, Evan following suit. Without knowing why, she broke into a run.

"Hey! Where are you going?" Evan was running beside her, laughing.

"I want to get into that water to make sure it's not just a mirage," Anne laughed. "Oh, this is so perfect! I've . . . so far, I've only seen the beach from a . . . a fancy hotel lounge!" She was out of breath, finding it harder than she'd imagined to run across the soft sand. As though it were the most natural thing in the world, Evan clasped her hand in his and they raced toward the water together.

When they reached the spot where the sand was damp and hard-packed, they dropped down, panting for breath. Evan let go of her hand. He sat up, propping himself up on one elbow. "I come here often," he said, "when I want to be really alone. It's too far away to be cluttered by the condominium crowd, and anyway, they spend most of their time on their balconies playing backgammon."

"Is that another of the games I'll have to learn to play?" Anne asked. "Today, I was supposed to become good enough at bridge to sit in when Mrs. Delon needs a fourth."

"You're being trained to be a perfect Delon," Evan said. Then, in a gesture so abrupt it seemed angry, he pulled off his shirt and tossed it aside. "You were anxious to test the water."

Anne nodded. But she was acutely conscious of the nearly naked male body beside her. As he carelessly tossed aside the brightly colored shirt, she admired the play of muscles in his chest and arms. A nervous thrill ran through her like a quick surge of electricity.

"Come on." Evan got to his feet.

Anne realized that he was waiting for her to remove the terrycloth coverup. The madcap feeling of freedom was gone. She felt shy and self-conscious, suddenly, aware that Evan was standing over her, looking down and waiting. Her fingers trembled as she untied the belt and slipped the wrap away from her shoulders, slowly getting her arms out of the sleeves. She wanted to toss the white beach coat aside as nonchalantly as Evan had disposed of his shirt, but the blue and white bikini looked and felt embarrassingly skimpy.

"You're beautiful, Anne. Why do you act as though you're ashamed to be seen?"

His words and the slow examination of his dark eyes added to her self-consciousness. He took a step toward her. Now his body was so close to her own that she could almost feel the heat of it.

"Beautiful," Evan repeated. "Put your shoulders back. Head high up in the air."

Anne laughed, but he must have sensed that the laugh was forced. Once again, she broke into a run, not stopping until she was splashing through the surf.

Evan was not far behind her. When the water slowed her down, he slid an arm around her waist, pulling her close to him so that their thighs touched as they walked. When the water was deep enough, he let his arm fall away from Anne's waist and made a sudden dive. Anne followed his move, emerging from her dive to find Evan's face just inches away from her own.

"It's warm," she said. She had not expected the ocean to be as caressingly warm as the sunlit beach.

Evan smiled, tossing his head back to get his wet curling hair out of his eyes. "Not warm enough," he said. It was all the warning he gave Anne. In the next instant, his arms were around her, pressing her so tight that her back arched and she lost her footing. He was holding her then, with his body warm and wet and intimate against her own.

"Let me up!" Anne demanded. "Evan, will you please . . . ?"

"Warm," he repeated insinuatingly. "Don't tell me you don't feel it, too." His face was pressed against Anne's, his lips murmuring into her ear, then his lips moved to cover Anne's in a wild, possessive kiss. There was no fighting against the vicelike grip of his muscular arms. He was stirring something primitive and uncontrollable in her. Yet, at the same time, she felt a rush of panic and struggled against him. When he released her mouth, she gasped, "You're insane! Let me . . . let me go!"

Still holding her tightly, Evan said thickly, "Are you going to try to tell me that was . . . distasteful to you? Oh, Anne, why do you keep deceiving yourself?"

Anne tore herself away from him, starting the water-slowed walk to the shore. "You really *do* think a lot of yourself, don't you? You . . ." She paused for a gasp of air. "You think you're absolutely . . . irresistible."

To her surprise, he burst out laughing.

"I don't like your games!" Anne cried. "I don't like your manners or your morals!" She was almost at the beach when she cried out, "And I don't like you!"

She could still hear him laughing when she went to find her straw bag and reached for the

brightly colored beach towel to put around
her. She rubbed herself dry in swift, furious
motions, ignoring Evan, who now stood beside her. Though he made no move to ap-
proach her, she could feel his presence bridge
the gap between them. His gaze was almost a
physical contact that burned into her flesh.

She turned away to slip into her terrycloth
robe, tying the belt with a savage tug. Stuffing
the damp towel into her beach bag, she said
coldly, "I'll drive you back now."

"I don't go for rides with people who dislike
me," he said, "nor with people who break
their promises."

"What did I ever promise you, Evan Forrester?"

"You have a short memory. I distinctly
heard you say that you'd share your beach
towel with me."

Anne grasped the handle of the straw bag
and turned to walk toward the car. "I suppose
you think that's funny."

"Don't you have any sense of humor?" Evan
reached out a staying hand.

"I don't want to talk to anybody as conceited
and presumptuous as you are! You have some
idea that all you have to do is snap your
fingers and every woman alive is going to fall
into your arms. Well, I'm not one of your easy
conquests, Mr. Forrester. Furthermore, I happen to be engaged. I'm going to marry a
decent man who'd . . . who would . . ." She
didn't quite know what Larry would do if he
had seen Evan kissing her and covering her

body with his own out in the water. She would never be able to explain it to this erratic character who leaped over walls and acted out his every impulse.

"I don't think Larry would challenge me to a duel," Evan said in an infuriatingly placid tone. "He might try to get me drummed out of the yacht club. And, of course, I'd be *persona non grata* around the Delons' place. Neither circumstance would be tragic." Evan paused. "Frankly, I can barely stand the people. Snobbish, maneuvering, stuffy hypocrites."

"You're unbelievable!", Anne cried. "Sneaking around behind Larry's back and then trying to undermine my . . ."

"Your what? Your undying adoration for that whole clan?" Evan reached out to touch Anne's wrist. "Sit down. Sit down for a minute and let me talk to you."

"I want to go back to the house."

"We just got here. And I'm not going to assail your prebridal innocence. You happen to be wrong in what you say about me, but that's not what I'm concerned about. I'm thinking about you."

"Thank you for your touching concern. If someone had seen you, half . . . half trying to drown me . . . attacking me like a . . ."

"Like a sex fiend," Evan conceded lightly. "All right, I had no right to do that. I'm not sorry I did, understand, but I suppose I did imperil your comfortable conquest."

He was outrageous. "My . . . what?"

"Here. Sit down and listen to me."

His fingers tightened on Anne's wrist and she found herself dropping to the sand, pulled by a force that she could have freed herself from but, somehow, didn't. She was curious, Anne told herself. She wanted to know why Evan kept maligning the family into which she was going to marry. She wanted . . . she didn't want . . .

Evan talked for a long time. He told Anne he couldn't believe she would marry a man who invariably said the right thing and did the right thing and was, consequently, as dull as dishwater.

Anne's indignant protest was waved down.

"The Delons are a dynasty, Anne. At least, they think of themselves that way. Look at Warren's wife, if you want a peek into your future. What's her name . . . ?" Evan snapped his fingers impatiently. "She has so little of her own personality left, if she ever had one, that I can't even think of her as a person. She's just an extension of the Delon household."

"But she and I are two different people," Anne protested. "And Larry and his brother couldn't be more different from each other.

"But they're both part of the same package deal, Anne. You're young and you're beautiful and you haven't, from the impression I've gotten . . . you haven't even begun to find out what life is all about. What *enjoying* life is all about."

"I'm just beginning to," Anne said defensively.

"The luxuries? The big houses, the yachts, the cushy hotels and the lavish parties?" Evan shook his head. He had seated himself a discreet distance from Anne, and one hand was making and then flattening little mounds of the white sand.

She forced herself to look away; even his hands had an erotic effect upon her. She remembered their touch and a tongue of flame flashed through her body.

"I can't believe that you'll sell yourself short like this."

"I don't suppose it's occurred to you that Larry is a fine, decent man. and that he loves me and has been very good to me and . . ."

"Anne?"

She stopped, aware once more of that penetrating stare. "What?"

"You haven't told me that you love him."

"That's assumed!" she countered. "Of course I love him. We're going to be married."

"And live happily ever after." Evan tossed a handful of sand onto the mound he had been piling up. "I could be wrong. I suppose I could be wrong."

"Well! That's the first time I've heard you admit to such a possibility!"

"But I don't think I am," Evan said. "And even if I were, I won't be a few years from now, unless you do what . . . what's her name . . . the other Mrs. Delon, has done. Resign yourself to . . ."

Anne felt a surge of shame run through her. How disloyal to Larry, how *terrible* to be sitting here and listening to this presumptuous outsider discuss her relationship with him.

"I don't want to hear anymore," she said suddenly. "How can you make such disparaging remarks about the Delons just because they happen to be . . . well off? You're hardly underprivileged. Next thing you know, you'll be telling me I'm out here on a secluded beach with you because you own a yacht that's bigger than the Delons'."

Evan shook his head. "My background is about as moneyed and glamorous as yours, Anne. I didn't have anything handed to me on a silver platter. My father was a struggling insurance salesman. I made it because I was tired of being at the mercy of people like the Delons. But I'm still considered beneath them, you know." Evan laughed shortly. "The nouveau riche are looked down upon. Almost as much as nice little office girls who nab one of the heirs to Delon and Withrow."

Why was he working so hard to shake her faith in Larry? What did he offer as an alternative? Moments of mindless passion, when he wasn't busy running after some other woman who was attracted by his impressive good looks? Anne rose to her feet again. "I haven't 'nabbed' anybody. I . . . someone fell in love with me and I . . ." She was angry with herself for the brief, unintentional hesitation before she said, "I love him, too."

Evan nodded. Wordlessly, he got up and walked with Anne to the white sports car. He opened the door and helped her into the driver's seat before walking around to take his place beside her.

Driving back to the Delons' house, Anne found the silence oppressive. She assured herself that it didn't matter. She had made a mistake in inviting Evan to come to the beach with her, a mistake she would not repeat.

They arrived at the entry gates to Evan's home first and Anne turned into his driveway. Evan finally broke the silence. "Thank you. I wasn't up to leaping the wall."

"And I'm not up to explaining what I'm doing out with you in Larry's car." Anne brought the Porsche to a stop in front of Evan's house, leaving the motor running. She wanted to say something to relieve the strained atmosphere. "Thank you for showing me the way."

"I wish I could," he said.

Anne frowned. Then, understanding his innuendo, she said, "I meant, to the beach. I wouldn't have found that one alone."

"Maybe you'll go back," Evan said. "Might run across each other there someday, you never know."

"If we do," Anne said, "I hope you'll remember that in a very short while I'm going to be a married woman."

"And behave accordingly," Evan said in a flat undertone. "And watch what I say."

"Yes." She was no longer angry with him. A sudden heaviness had overcome her. She wished . . . she wanted him to . . . what did

she want? Why didn't he get out of the car?
The silence lengthened. She did not want to
look at him and averted her face. She was
aware that he was moving closer to her. He
slid his left arm in back of her and gently
cupped her chin with the other hand, forcing
her eyes to meet his. Before she had had a
chance to protest, he had drawn her closely to
him and kissed her firmly on the mouth. The
kiss deepened and, almost of their own volition, her lips parted to receive it. She was unaware that she sighed as he drew away.

"That's just a sample," he said calmly.
"Unfortunately, I am sailing with Inez tomorrow, but perhaps the day after?"

Before Anne could answer, he had leaped
out of the car and slammed the door behind
him. His face by the open car window was
mocking. "Until then, my little neighbor, *stay
warm.*"

Anne could think of no suitable reply. She
revved the motor and shot out into the road.
But she could see in the car mirror the reflec-
tion of Evan standing in the driveway. His
expression as he watched her leave was infuriatingly amused.

She spent the rest of the day and the evening trying to understand the significance of
"*Stay warm.*" And even during her daily late-
afternoon telephone call from Larry, she did
not escape from the tone in which the phrase
was said. "*Stay warm.*" Was Evan reminding
her of the moments in which he had clasped

her in his arms and forced her body against his? Tossing and turning in an attempt to fall asleep that night, Anne wondered if she had read something into Evan's comment that hadn't been intended. She remembered his mocking expression, and her face burned. He had only been teasing her, and yet he had generated a raging heat inside her, a heat that threatened to consume her if she were not careful. She must at all costs avoid this arrogant, conceited man and return to sane, wonderful, dependable Larry. Yet somehow, the prospect had never appeared more bleak.

Chapter Six

*H*ow could paradise have turned into hell?
Anne woke up to a day of emotional turmoil,
beginning with her first look outside her bedroom window. Inez was waiting next to the
driveway for Evan to pick her up for their
sailing date. She looked stunning in tight
white designer jeans and a flimsy coral-
colored tank top that showed the impudent lift
of her breasts. Her blonde hair looked tousled
and, in the bright morning sunshine, like a
golden mane. As Evan's unpretentious little
car pulled up, she ran toward it, smiling radi-
antly. Anne couldn't see Evan's face, but she
imagined that he was smiling, too, looking
forward to a full day with this stunning young
creature.

Jealousy racked Anne—a totally unreasoning jealousy. The envy was intensified by
feelings of guilt. By what right did she resent
Evan's relationship with Inez? She had to
keep reminding herself why she had come to
Maui. But reminders paled beside the less
vague physical memories of Evan Forrester.
She found herself standing before the mirror,

striking provocative poses as she surveyed her figure and compared herself with Inez. There was a heady excitement in recalling the possessive pressure of Evan's lips devouring hers, the sensuous shape of his mouth, the way his raven hair curled at the nape of his neck and fell over his forehead. The memory of his lovemaking brought the blood pounding to her temples. Before the dresser mirror once more, she touched her breasts, wondering what it would be like to feel Evan's hands caressing them.

It was an obsession and an insanity. She must exert every effort to put Evan out of her mind. She would get dressed and go downstairs to face a day in which there would be no hope of seeing the man who had so infuriated her and at the same time possessed her every sense.

While Anne was finishing her breakfast, Mrs. Delon joined her in the solarium for coffee. She rattled on about a party she was giving for Guadalupe, one of the maids. "There's no better way to keep the help happy than to let them use the grounds for a birthday do," she said. She took pains to let Anne know that she was being democratic, but, at the same time, knew where to draw the line. "We'll all make an appearance," she said. "And then we'll find someplace else to be. It's something you want to learn, Anne. Who they are and who we are."

Anne's coffee cup rattled as she placed it in its saucer. She hadn't meant to come that close to slamming the cup down. Mrs. Delon was obviously making a reference to the amount of time Anne spent with Amalia and Guadalupe. They were bright, friendly young women who, though not of Hawaiian decent, had taught her how to braid leis and filled her in on all the special island traditions. She enjoyed their company, when they could spare time from their duties, more than she enjoyed the process of being taught how to be a proper Delon.

As usual, Anne wasn't given a chance to express her feelings. "But we have more important things on our social calendar. You haven't given me your guest list yet, you know," she reminded Anne.

Anne nodded, depressed by the thought of phoning her father and the few old friends who probably should be invited. She hadn't gone to see her father before leaving for Hawaii; the decision to go to Maui had been sudden, and Larry had kept her busy buying a wardrobe and making other preparations. She had phoned him from Chicago, but her father was in one of his taciturn moods and had barely responded to her announcement that she was getting married. She had all but lost touch with most of her old school chums, and Larry would probably take a dim view of inviting the casual friends she had made at the Delon and Withrow office. In any event, employees would probably have been socially unacceptable in Mrs. Delon's book.

Listlessly, Anne promised to supply the

names as soon as possible. Why didn't she assert herself? It was hardly because of Mrs. Delon's overpowering personality or because of her own feeling of inadequacy. Somehow, she couldn't summon the mental energy to make her feelings about the wedding known. Her thoughts were elsewhere this morning . . . on a secluded beach . . . on a small sail boat . . .

It didn't seem possible that the day's events could go downhill from there, but they did. First, there was the phone call to her father. He had never been a demonstrative man. Anne had always known that he loved her in a quiet, uncommunicative way. But this morning he must have been in one of his gloomy states. "Aren't you happy for me, Dad?" Anne asked him in what sounded to her own ears as a childishly plaintive voice. "Don't you want to be here at my wedding?"

"I haven't even met the man," her father growled. "And I can't go flying off to some place I've never even heard of. Not in June, that's for sure. I have my lodge reunion in June. Chairman of the hospitality committee, going to Chicago." He made Chicago sound as though it were on the other side of the world.

"Well, try," Anne said. She blinked back incipient tears. "You know I'd like you to be here."

"All those rich people." There was a long pause. "Probably have to buy a new suit . . ."

Anne knew he would never come. She felt

heavy-hearted and in need of a good cry when she dropped the receiver back to its cradle.

She got more enthusiasm from Pam and Emily, with whom she had gone to business school. But Pam was preparing for a wedding of her own and Emily had just gotten a new job that was going to take her to Alaska. They made happy small talk, but Anne knew they would send gifts and regrets. She wished she had not made the calls.

Had she really been so busy, climbing up out of the poverty and drabness of her home town, that she was virtually without close friends? Since Larry's proposal, her whole life somehow revolved only around him. Around him and . . .

Anne shuddered herself free of the thought of Evan. That afternoon, she gave Mrs. Delon the names and addresses of the three people she had contacted, adding her doubts that they would be able to attend the wedding.

Mrs. Delon lifted her brows and said, "Well. That may be a bit difficult to explain to our other guests, but I suppose we can manage." She was obviously relieved. At least the Delons would be spared the embarrassment of introducing the "wrong people" to their host of friends.

Later, Veronica joined Anne at the pool. "I know how you feel, Anne. I only had fourteen people at my wedding. It was like sharing the most important day in my life with hundreds of strangers," she commented.

Anne didn't mention that Veronica's friends were probably more acceptable. She came from a successful if not socially prominent family. But, of course, she too had probably been reminded that being married to a Delon was a privilege. She seemed to want to befriend Anne, even offer herself as a confidante. But Anne sensed that Veronica was too timid to say anything that might rock the boat. She squeezed Anne's hand as they were going back into the house later, as if to convey the message that she understood, but that it was too late for her to join Anne in bucking Millicent Delon's control over the family.

Anne's frustration rankled all day. She was pacing her bedroom floor when Larry made his daily telephone call. Anne exchanged the usual greetings with him, heard him tell her that he loved her, told him dutifully that she missed him, too, and was listening to him tell her that he hoped he would be able to come to Maui within a week or ten days, when she cut in: "Larry? Can't you get here sooner?"

"You know the turmoil the market's in," he said impatiently.

She didn't know. The market was always in some sort of turmoil that she didn't comprehend, and Larry's first devotion, it was beginning to seem, was to the Delon and Withrow clients. "If you can't come here, then . . . let me come to Chicago," she said. She wanted to escape more than his mother. She wanted to free herself of her insane obsession with Evan Forrester.

"You know that's impossible, darling! I hate being separated from you, but we'll have the rest of our lives together. And you must have millions of details to work out for our wedding."

"I was thinking . . ." Anne was on the verge of tears again. "Larry, couldn't we be married there?"

There was a heavy silence. "You know that's out of the question," Larry said finally. "You must be . . . in a terrible mood to even suggest such a thing. Is something wrong?"

She tried to tell him, but her explanation would have been too vague. His mother had hardly mistreated Anne. She was just being herself, and to Mrs. Delon that meant staging an important social event that the family's friends would talk about for years to come. Nor could Anne tell Larry that she felt bored and lonely and out of place. And above all, she couldn't tell him that another man had stirred volcanic emotions in her, emotions that filled her with a fear of her own nature.

"Maybe we shouldn't have been apart at this time," Larry said soothingly. "I wish I could be with you, dear. Hang on. I'll make it up to you on our honeymoon."

They exchanged the usual sign-off phrase: "I love you." Anne's response sounded stilted. Even Larry's words came through the receiver sounding mechanical. She had accomplished absolutely nothing. Worse, she suspected that Larry was concerned about her and would probably phone his mother.

What could be done to help Anne enjoy her stay? He would count on his mother's enormous ego. Mrs. Delon would find it unthinkable that one of her house guests was not having the time of her life.

Honeymoon. Larry had said he would make it up to her on their honeymoon. The thought flooded over Anne like water breaking free from a dam that had suddenly burst. She had been so carried away by the surprising event that had changed her life, so busy listening to the envious comments of her co-workers at the office, that she had not really thought of the full implication of being married to Larry. He was always kind and considerate, but she had not, until this past week, been able to compare his kisses with those of another man. Now it struck her that Larry's embraces had never left her breathless, never set her heart to beating wildly. With him she had never felt the need to be crushed closer, until their bodies fused as one. What would it be like to have him possess her on their wedding night? If the thrill of his arms around her failed to send rapturous quivers through her body, would she have to pretend to preserve his ego? Would she always be thinking of a dark, vital stranger who could send her from fury to ecstacy with just a brush of his hand?

Anne resumed her caged-animal walk around her room. She tried to recall her joy at having a man as important, yes, as attractive, as Larry ask her to be his wife. She looked around at her luxurious surroundings, telling herself that all this beauty and comfort was hers for life, given to her by a man who had repeatedly said that he adored her.

It didn't help. Anne had to get away from herself and from her racking doubts. She walked downstairs in search of someone to talk with. Someone . . . anyone.

Mrs. Delon and Veronica had gone shopping. The maids were busy. Anne returned to her room, changed into her blue and white bikini, and decided that a long swim might refresh her body and clear her mind.

She was no less tranquil in her thoughts, no less aware of the awakened demands of her body when she emerged from the pool shortly afterward. She stretched herself out on one of the lounges, letting the sun warm her skin. She had almost fallen asleep when she heard a guttural throat-clearing sound. She opened her eyes to see Warren Delon lumbering toward her.

As always, he held a highball glass in one of his big hands. From his unsteady walk, Anne surmised that he had emptied more than one glass already. He waved at her groggily. "Hi. Everyone seems to have deserted us."

Anne sat up, uncomfortable under Warren's bleary examination of her outstretched form.

"No drink?" Warren hovered over her, gargantuan in his loose navy blue lounging robe. "I can remedy that in a hurry."

"No, thank you. I was . . . just getting ready to go upstairs."

"That's not very friendly," Warren said.

She tried to think of a logical excuse. "I have some calls to make. And . . . a letter to finish." Anne got up from the lounge, swinging her legs over to one side and moving away from Warren.

"Not very friendly at all," he repeated. "If we're going to be relatives, honey, we really ought to get to know each other." Warren took a few steps toward her. "I hear you're not enjoying your stay. We could . . . have a few drinks together here. Better still, get dressed and go somewhere interesting."

"Who told you I'm not enjoying my stay?" Anne asked. She felt a revulsion at being so close to Warren. His insinuating tone was even more unnerving.

"Slip of the tongue," he admitted. Apparently Larry *had* called his mother and the news had been relayed to Warren and Veronica. "No secrets in our family. Tight little group."

"Maybe I've been misunderstood," Anne said. "I just . . . told Larry that I miss him." Resentment stirred inside her. The Delons were, indeed, "a tight little group." It angered Anne to think there had been a family discussion about her.

"Oh, come off it, honey. We both know what you see in dear ole Lawrence." Warren imitated his mother's inflection in pronouncing his brother's name. "You're too young and pretty to fall for that stuffed shirt. Everybody knows what his big attraction is."

"Really! And what's that?"

Warren's dissipated face widened into a sly

grin. He waved an arm to indicate their cushy surroundings. "I'm a big boy, honey. And I don't blame you, understand, but don't tell me you're pining your little heart out. I've watched you with Mr. Adonis next door. Sorry he left you stranded today."

Anne's legs were shaking under her. Warren had moved closer and she took a faltering step backward. "I don't know what you're talking about."

"No, of course not." The thick sarcasm was accentuated by the disdainful expression in his closely set, pink-rimmed eyes. "Hon, you ought to know when you're in over your head. You're young and you're sexy. You like to play. There's no harm in that." Warren stooped to place his glass on a small metal table next to the lounge chair. "And you ought to know by now that I'm with you. I put up with a lot of tripe for the same reasons, kiddo. I like money and I like to play."

Anne stood immobilized. Warren added, "You might have more fun if you had an ally around the place, hon. A sympathetic buddy who thinks you're a living doll. A real . . . living . . . doll." As he spoke, Warren lurched forward, enfolding Anne in a smothering bear hug that nearly threw her off balance. His arms pulled her against his flabby body, and before she could protest, his mouth met hers in a wet, demanding kiss.

He pinned her arms to her sides. Anne struggled desperately against the unwelcome embrace. She made a violent lunge, jerking herself free of the contact with Warren's lips. She was gasping, making sounds like a panting animal, her heart hammering wildly, her senses swimming with nausea. "Get away from me!" she managed to cry. "Get your . . ."

Warren didn't release her. He placed his mouth against the side of Anne's head and murmured, "We could have so much fun together, baby. We could . . ."

She was ready to kick him, loathing the bruising hold that squeezed the air from her lungs. She was just about to break his hold with one well-aimed jab with her knee, when Warren's body stiffened. His arms dropped to his sides, releasing her. "Better watch it. We've got company," he muttered.

He turned away from Anne, retrieving his drink, and moving toward the house in a faked attempt at nonchalance. Anne was left shaking, trying to catch her breath. Now she saw what Warren had seen over her shoulder while he was pressing his lips against her ear. Inez Carruthers was walking across the patio. Apparently wrapped up in her own thoughts, she paused only to stare at Anne. For a long, searching moment, the beautiful blonde eyed Anne with a contemptuous look that spoke volumes. There was a suspenseful silence.

Legs trembling, Anne waited until the silence grew too embarrassing to be endured. She didn't owe Inez an explanation. Surely, whatever Inez had seen, she must know that Anne had not welcomed that disgusting assault by Larry's brother. "Hello," Anne managed to say. She had to fill the oppressive quiet somehow. "You're back early," she added.

She could not have said anything worse. "Too early for you?" Inez asked snidely. She stared at Anne for a few seconds more, her eyes filled with malice. Then she tossed her head and marched toward the door.

Anne couldn't run after her, trying to explain. Anything she said now would only compound her senseless feeling of guilt. Furthermore, considering Inez's tightly set mouth and her furious pace, it had been an unforgivable mistake to mention her early return. Perhaps something had gone wrong with her projected all-day sailing date with Evan. Anne waited until she was sure Inez had had time to get to her room before making her own way into the house and up the stairs.

Sickened by the incident, she felt as though she wanted to take a bath. There was no doubt in her mind that the scene Inez had walked in on would be reported. *Tight little group.* They had discussed Anne in detail before her arrival. Evan had made that clear. They had talked about her today. Larry had been responsible for that. She was tired of living in this artificial atmosphere, this gilt-edged goldfish bowl without any privacy.

Her insides churning, Anne yearned for the sanctity of her own little apartment where she could do as she pleased and be herself. She knew Larry had probably meant well, but she was angered by his phone call to his mother.

The whole charade of the big wedding reception needled her, and now Warren's insinuations, Warren's insulting attempt to use her as a cheap, available object had further upset her.

She tried to cry, but she was too confused and stirred up for the relief of tears. In her frustration, petty complaints ran through her mind: in her own place, she could stamp into her tiny kitchen and fix herself a cup of coffee or even a drink. Here, she would find herself being waited on and observed by a corps of servants. And she couldn't bear the thought of talking to a stranger now. Yet she had to talk to someone. Someone who would understand, someone who would care.

Ironically, the one person in the household with whom she had some rapport was Veronica. Tell *her* what had happened and how she felt? Complain to Mrs. Delon? Phone Larry? The last person on earth she could talk to now was Larry. There was something terribly wrong about not being able to reach out to the man with whom she was going to share the rest of her life.

There was also something terribly wrong with thinking about Evan Forrester. He had created as many frustrations and annoyances as all of the Delons put together. But much of what he had said had been right. And suddenly Anne wanted to talk to him, to pour out her feelings. It was unthinkable, of course. She had already made a potential enemy of Inez. To contact Evan now could only prove what Warren had said about her and create a deadly tension between herself and the Delons' other house guest. No secrets in this house!

It was unthinkable. But by the time the sun had set, the desire to communicate with Evan had become a driving urge. Anne couldn't bear to face the family at the dinner table. She sent word by way of Guadalupe that she was not feeling well and was going to get to sleep early.

It was an unnecessary alibi. Anne learned from a call, shortly afterward, that there wasn't going to be a family dinner that night. Mrs. Delon phoned to report that she and Veronica were having dinner with friends in Lahaina. Inez had already agreed to join them there; would Anne like to drive up with her?

Anne used a headache as her excuse. "I'm sorry, but I don't really feel up to it, Mrs. Delon."

"Anything I can do? If you're really ill, my dear . . ."

"I've taken a couple of aspirin," Anne lied. "I may have gotten too much sun. If I get to sleep early, I know I'll be fine in the morning."

Her excuse was accepted. "We'll be returning quite late," Mrs. Delon said. "Do see that the help gets whatever you want gotten. I'm afraid you're going to be in charge. Warren's turned me down, too . . . going to a party or some such thing."

There were more polite inanities and then

Mrs. Delon rang off. A flutter of apprehension ran through Anne. She became especially nervous when she saw Inez roar away from the house in one of the family's fleet of cars a few minutes later. If she had been asked to invite Anne to come along, she had conveniently forgotten to do so. That left Anne alone, except for the servants, with Warren Delon. She felt foolishly paranoid as she turned the inside lock on her bedroom door. Not long afterward, she heard a motor being started up and looked out her window to see Warren's Mercedes going down the long driveway. She breathed a sigh of relief. Now she could go downstairs without fear of running into him.

By eight thirty, her restlessness was unbearable. The events of this nightmarish day preyed upon her mind, but she found herself thinking of something else. *Evan* touching her face, letting her know with his eyes that he was holding back a more tempestuous contact. *Evan* telling her to stay warm. She felt his hands on her body now, smelled the spicy male scent of his cologne as he pressed his face against hers. *Evan. Evan, Evan, Evan.* She didn't want to think about him, but he would not leave her alone.

Sometime after nine, Anne strolled out to the garden, listening for music from beyond the lava-stone wall. There was no sound except that of the palm fronds overhead, stirred by a caressingly warm breeze. Perfume of plumeria lay heavy on the air, filling her senses, crowding her mind with romantic thoughts that refused to go away.

At a few minutes before ten, feeling guilty and not knowing what she would say when and if Evan answered his phone, Anne was listening to a repeated ringing sound. Her hand trembled as she pressed the receiver to her ear; her breath was coming fast, not filling her lungs with enough air. She was almost ready to hang up, almost relieved that there had been no response, when Evan's deep, rich voice said, "Aloha."

Anne hesitated for a second. "Evan?"

"Yes?"

"Evan, this is . . . Anne Beal. Next door."

"Oh. Oh, hello." He sounded pleased. "I should have recognized your voice. How are you doing?"

He had made it easy for her. If he had sounded stiff, or if he had asked why she was calling, she would have been unable to go on. "I'm all right," Anne said. "I guess."

"You don't sound too chipper. But I'm glad to hear from you. In fact, I've been sitting here all alone in my little aerie and thinking about you."

Anne brightened, more confident now. "About me? What were you thinking?"

"I was thinking that if you weren't surrounded by watchdogs, I'd like to leap over the wall and come to see you."

"I'm not surrounded by anybody," Anne told him.

"Really? You're alone, too?" Evan's mellow

laugh came through the receiver like heady wine. "So, naturally, you called me. I'm delighted. What are you doing, besides hearing me ask what you're doing?"

"I'm just . . . I just thought I'd . . ." Words deserted her. Just hearing his voice had started a quivering sensation that made it difficult to sound as casual as she had hoped to sound. "I just needed to talk to you," Anne finally said in a burst of honesty.

"There *is* something wrong."

"No, no, no, it's nothing, really. I had . . . you know, one of those days?"

"We all have them." He sounded genuinely sympathic. "I've predicted that you're going to have a lot of them. Can we talk?"

"We're talking." Why did she keep saying foolish things, afraid to tell Evan what was really bothering her? "I'm glad I caught you at home."

"No, I meant can we really talk? You could come here."

"You know better than that."

"Why not? I'll get some good background music on the stereo, pour us each a glass of sherry, and we'll have . . ."

"I can't go there," Anne said. Somehow, the urge to be with him, not just talking to him at a distance, even this short distance, was compelling. "That's all I'd need. To wait until the family gets out of the house and go running to see the next-door neighbor."

"The best possible time," Evan said cheerfully. Then his voice sobered. "I didn't have one of my better days either, Anne. Why can't we get together and exchange condolences? Afraid of what somebody's going to think?"

She had to admit that this was true. "It wouldn't look good."

"But you want to? You want to come over and be with me?"

Evan was speaking in the low, seductive tone that demanded a warm response from her. But he was being his egotistical self, too, reminding Anne that she was not immune to his male magnetism. "I'd like to see you," Anne admitted, "but I've had enough complications for one day."

Evan encouraged her to tell him what had happened. He did more than encourage, he insisted. Somehow, she could only tell him about the frustrating telephone calls to her father and her friends. How could she possibly verbalize her experience with Warren Delon? He would probably learn about it later from Inez. Anne was sure that Inez's version wouldn't be the same as her own, but she couldn't bring herself to talk about it now.

When it was Evan's turn to relate why this had been a considerably less than perfect day, he started out by saying, "I went sailing with Inez, you know."

Anne waited for him to go on, but apparently he thought better of it. Maybe there were things he didn't want to talk about, either. "We got back early, and I tried to get some work done, but I just wasn't geared for studying environmental impact reports. Do you want to know what I was really thinking about when the phone rang?"

"You said you were thinking about me," Anne said. She was beginning to feel better, even sounding mischievous. "But you only said that to cheer me up."

"I'd like to cheer you up," Evan replied. "Right here, on the sofa beside me. I don't know that you'd do much laughing, but I know you wouldn't be miserable. And you really want to know exactly what I was thinking?"

"Only the good parts," Anne teased.

"I was thinking," Evan said slowly and clearly, "of what it would be like to make love to you."

Anne sucked in her breath. She was too stunned to say anything in reply, but the words had fired her senses. She could no longer think about whether it was right or wrong; she could no longer lie to herself. Just listening to Evan's voice during the past few minutes had filled her with sweet torment.

"Are you still with me?" she heard Evan say.

"I'm still here. And I wish . . ."

"Yes, Anne?"

"I wish you wouldn't play games with me."

"When I took you into my arms yesterday, when I kissed you, did you think I was playing games? You're a grown woman. Can't you tell the difference? Don't you know when a man really wants you?"

"Evan . . ." She couldn't tell him that she

wanted him, too. He was capable of mercurial changes. Maybe he was just using his practiced techniques of seduction; one more notch on his belt. After she had given herself to him, at risk of losing a man who really loved her, he would go on to his next conquest. And he really hadn't offered her anything or asked her for anything. He had just said he wondered what their lovemaking would be like. Anne steeled herself. "I don't think we should be talking like this."

He virtually exploded, his voice harsh and angry. "Talk about game-playing! You didn't call here tonight to tell me that your father doesn't understand you. Or that your friends probably won't make it to your wedding! Suddenly you're Miss Prim and Proper again! And I'm not very fond of teases, Anne. You sound miserable. And you don't have the guts to face facts. You're no more in love with Larry Delon than with the man in the moon. You know that sparks fly between us. You wouldn't have called me tonight if you hadn't wanted to see me. And you didn't want to see me to discuss . . ."

"I called you because I needed to talk to a friend!" Anne's voice broke. The tears she would have welcomed all day finally came. "A friend," she repeated. "Someone who understands and . . . doesn't want anything from you."

"What do you think I want? A quick one night stand? I misunderstood you. I thought you had more respect for me than that."

His searing tone brought a defensive response from Anne. "You're asking me to respect you, but you completely forget that I'm . . ."

"That you're engaged to be married. How many times will I have to listen to that holier-than-thou routine of yours? Why didn't you call your future husband tonight and cry on *his* shoulder?"

"I won't listen to you . . ."

"You *will* listen!" Evan commanded. "Don't hang up, because if you do, I'll be over there in five minutes pounding on your door. I may do that anyway. Now, will you listen?"

"What do you want to say?" Anne said. She felt chastened and, at the same time, almost afraid of what Evan might do. If the Delons came home to find him here . . .

"You're not in love with Larry. I don't know that you're in love with me, but you're a fool and a hypocrite if you deny the attraction between us. And I've had it with fools and hypocrites and women who don't know what they want." Evan had been shouting, but now he paused and then lowered his voice. "They're even worse than those who don't know that they're not wanted, *except* for game playing. And by games I mean boat racing and tennis."

He hadn't mentioned Inez specifically; earlier, he had either been too much of a gentleman or he had found the subject too distasteful for discussion. But Anne couldn't help thinking that he had unconsciously explained why he and Inez had not stayed out longer today and why she had come home looking upset. What if he was sincere? What if he really meant what he'd just said about the attraction that existed between them? "There's . . . there's a rapport," Anne conceded. "but that doesn't mean that we . . ."

"What *does* it mean?" Evan wanted to know. "And it's more than just a physical thing. You've got to know that. Anne? Come over and let's talk."

She was tempted. She wanted to run into his arms and have him hold her as though he would never let her go. She wanted to wrap her own arms around him and pull his face close to hers, to feel him press his hand against the small of her back, and mold her body against his. But she couldn't! She couldn't! "I can't come there, Evan. There's enough turmoil stirred up around here now without my going to visit you at night. Especially after I bowed out of an invitation by pretending I had a severe headache." She was admitting to Evan that she was capable of social lies. Did he think she was also lying to him? "I only hope you'll believe . . . that you'll believe me when I say . . ." She was lost in a maze of confusion.

"*Say it!*" Evan ordered.

Anne's voice was a near whisper as she said, "I'd like to, Evan. I'd like to be with you tonight."

He didn't persist. "I won't pressure you. Maybe you have to fight it out with yourself, I don't know. But if you change your mind, call me back, please. I'll be sitting right here hoping you come to your senses . . . and thinking about you."

"*I was wondering what it would be like to make love to you*—" Remembrance of his admission rekindled Anne's desire. She closed her eyes and saw the planes of his rugged, sensitive face, the deep black eyes that lit up with fire when he was angry or when he moved to crush her lips with his. "I'll be thinking about you, too, Evan," she said in spite of herself.

He was quiet for a moment and then he said, "Anne, this is ridiculous. We're two adults. We're within a few hundred yards of each other. We want and need each other. Why can't we . . . ?"

"You said that maybe I had to fight it out with myself," Anne reminded him. "I do. I don't like sneaking around and I don't like telling lies and I don't like being a . . . a tease. Evan . . . more than anything else right now, I need you to understand. I'm confused. I'm so mixed up that I . . . I can't . . ." Her voice broke.

"I keep forgetting that you don't know very much about men. You couldn't have, getting yourself swept into your situation. You really don't have any experience, do you?" His voice was unexpectedly gentle.

"Zero," Anne confessed.

"Good heavens. I didn't think girls like you existed anymore. Tomorrow, Anne. Tomorrow we've got to talk. I'm going to come by for you early. Be outside at seven. We'll get off to an early start."

"I . . . may not be up when Mrs. Delon gets home. She won't be awake that early. I can't just . . ."

"I don't want to hear any more about Millicent!" Evan exclaimed. "But if it makes your escape any easier, she's been hounding me about getting you started on sailing lessons. Leave a note."

"That's . . . what we're going to be doing? Sailing?" Evan had spoken so forcefully that she didn't have the strength to argue with him. Besides, her heart leaped at the thought of seeing him early the next morning. "I mean . . . I'm only asking because I was wondering what to wear."

"Wear whatever goes on and off easily," Evan murmured. "And, yes, we're going to be sailing. At least part of the time." He laughed suddenly.

His "Good night, luv" was like a sensuous caress that left Anne almost too limp to repeat, "Good night, Evan," and to thank him for listening to her woes.

Over and over, before she was finally able to fall asleep, Anne let every word Evan had said to her run through her mind like an endlessly repeating tape. Was he really thinking about her, too? Thinking of the most intimate closeness a man and woman could possibly share?

Anne's conscience imposed itself once or

twice. But the excitement of being wanted by Evan Forrester erased everything else, everyone else from her thoughts. Maybe by tomorrow morning she would come to her senses. But tonight, until sleep claimed her, Anne surrendered herself to delicious fantasies, the sort of wild dreams, she thought, a woman might have if she were insanely in love.

Chapter Seven

They had skirted the larger yachts that lay at anchor outside the harbor, among them the Delons' yawl and Evan's larger motor schooner, then waved and shouted "Alo-o-ha!" to passengers who were boarding launches alongside a huge white cruise ship.

"I'm glad the cloud cover's burned off early," Evan said. "Those people only have about six hours on Maui. It's good that they'll have sunshine."

"Good we've got it, too," Anne said happily. She was seated in the well of Evan's small sloop, leaning against Evan's bare legs as he sat at the tiller.

It was one of those glorious mornings that travel writers try to describe only to find that words elude them. The sea was calm and incredibly blue, the bright morning sunlight reflecting on its surface in flashes of gold. The shoreline was necklaced with modern condominiums, but the intrusion of buildings was softened by lavish plantings of palms and banana trees and flowering shrubs.

"It's so beautiful," Anne said lazily. "And this is so exciting."

"It'll be more exciting when I start teaching you how to sail into the wind," Evan promised. "We'll follow the shoreline. Safe and sound."

Did he think that she was concerned? Oh, it was a very small boat and a very large ocean, but Anne felt perfectly at home. Evan was in his element here, and she had total confidence in his skill as a sailor. His strength, both of mind and of body, inspired total confidence.

With the sail barely flapping in the gentle breeze that propelled them, it was a peaceful, though surprisingly swift, passage away from the harbor, away, Anne thought contentedly, from all the rest of the people in the world.

Yet there was an electric tension in the air. Try as she might, Anne could not forget the way Evan had talked about lovemaking the night before. Had he only been making idle conversation? she wondered. Had he changed his mind, or would he really try to seduce her today? Perhaps he had decided that toying with the affections of a soon-to-be-married woman was not a wise idea. Luckily for her peace of mind, Anne was given little time to ponder these disturbing thoughts.

There were no other boats visible when Evan began his instructions. And it was fun, Anne discovered. She was quickly acquainted with sailing terminology, given briefings about offshore and onshore winds, taught the intricacies of the *Leimomi's* rigging, and how to use her body to throw weight to port or starboard in maneuvering the little sloop. With Evan still at the tiller, she had the thrill of changing sails at his brisk orders. Evan brought the sloop about and they practiced beating back, with Anne shifting her position at every command: "Starboard . . . come about . . . port. Very nice, Anne. That's the idea. Okay, here we go again . . . starboard . . . port . . ."

Her hair was hopelessly windblown and her face was wet with salt spray. I probably look a mess, Anne thought. But she grinned back at Evan happily. And after a few hours, tired but glowing with a sense of new accomplishment, she was glad to rejoin Evan in the cramped little well. He let her take the tiller, then, as they sailed easily up the coast. Several times, still giving her instructions, Evan's hand covered Anne's and she was exhilarated by even that brief contact. They couldn't avoid being close together in the tiny space, but there was a naturalness as well as a degree of excitement in the press of bodies. It seemed to Anne that there was no other world but this. Oh, there was, she knew, but she didn't want to think about it now. She wished that these moments could extend themselves and go on forever.

But time flew, instead. "Time for lunch," Evan announced. He left Anne in charge of the tiller while he stepped down to the tiny cabin with its miniature galley, returning with ham-on-rye sandwiches, paper plates filled with German potato salad and icy Hawaiian beers.

Anne ate ravenously, her appetite increased by the fresh sea air. "You think of everything, don't you?," she said, munching unceremoniously on a dill pickle. "My compliments to the chef. Was that you?"

"My housekeeper," Evan said. "Billie Kanahele. Going on seventy, but you ought to see *her* on this little tub."

"You've taught her to sail, too?"

Evan grinned and shook his head. "You don't teach Hawaiians to sail. You learn from them."

They eased into a conversation about Billie and about Po, who took care of Evan's garden, pool, and tennis court, but would soon be leaving to attend the university in Honolulu. "He's Billie's grandson. A great guy, but too popular with the girls at the Maui discos. He'll go crazy in the big city. I hope he gets some studying done."

Although he didn't say so, Anne gathered that the people who ran Evan's household were regarded more as friends and family than as servants. She suspected that the young man's education was going to be financed by Evan and that the reason Evan could leave his building and developing projects to others was that he had developed in his employees a strong loyalty, based on his attitude. He was a wealthy man, but a far cry from the Delons, whose generosity was studied, and who never let their servants forget that they were exactly that, menial help.

By late afternoon, sailing placidly with the wind, they had traded anecdotes about their growing-up years, finding them not too dissimilar. Evan's parents, like Anne's father, were kind, well-meaning people, but he and they had never been able to communicate or feel close to one another. He had bought them a home in a California retirement community several years before and they were apparently contented. "I get a weekly letter," Evan said, "reporting on my mother's bingo games and my father's luck at fishing. I fly to see them at Christmastime. Observe all the other holidays like a dutiful son. But I can't say that I have a strong, warm sense of family." He raised an eyebrow and grimaced. "Maybe that's why I'm such a cold character."

"But you're not!" Anne protested. "You're . . ."

"Warm," Evan said. His hand rubbed the nape of Anne's neck affectionately.

A silence fell between them, each thinking private thoughts. Was Evan remembering last night's conversation? He kept massaging her neck, his other hand guiding the small boat back toward the harbor.

"We're going back?" Anne asked.

"Don't you want to?"

"No. No, this has been so beautiful. It's been such a perfect day."

"It's far from over," Evan said quickly. "I was thinking we'd be more comfortable aboard the *Sapphire*."

"Your . . . that big, beautiful yacht we passed this morning?"

"Mmm-hmm. We can stay aboard for dinner. Play music. Watch the sun set and the moon rise. But don't expect to get waited on. I've got a crew of three young locals, but they've got shore leave until morning."

Anne tensed. "You arranged that?"

"It didn't take much arranging. They're always delighted to get shore leave."

"Always?" The word threw a crimp into the perfection of the moment. "Always," Anne repeated. A bitterness had crept into her tone. This was no special invitation, it was a common one. Only a romantic fool would think otherwise. Anne edged forward in the crowded space, moving away from Evan's touch. Her eyes caught the flash of the sun on the diamond that adorned her left hand. Larry didn't deserve this. She didn't deserve it either.

Evan must have understood what she was thinking. "I've invited my housekeeper and her grandson aboard twice in the past week. And business friends. And . . ."

"And Inez Carruthers," Anne added. She regretted using the name. Evan would assume jealousy instead of resentment.

"No, as a matter of fact, she invited herself," Evan said. "Oh, look, Anne, I've had enough of this cat and mouse game. Last night I told you that I want you. I couldn't have been more explicit. If you didn't want me, you wouldn't have come along this morning."

"Maybe I didn't know that this is a regular routine with you!" Anne cried. "And maybe I'm particular about which act I follow!"

"Meaning what?"

"Meaning that if the Delons had ten female house guests, I might be number nine or ten on your list!" Anne started to leap up, losing her balance and falling back against Evan's legs. She tried to regain her composure, stumbling again.

"Sit down!" he barked. "I told you Inez invited herself. I didn't dismiss the crew. I had the guys join us in a nice, friendly hand of poker. On deck. In broad daylight. Not in the master cabin. Why do you think she went into a purple snit and made me so mad I ran her home?"

His explanation made sense. It accounted for Inez's early and angry return home. But Anne's confused emotions had been stirred. "Don't tell me I'm the first woman you've ever asked aboard."

"No, you're not!" Evan stormed. "I'm a man, not a eunuch. I've never told you I'm an innocent little choir boy. But I never pretended those other times were for anything but . . . temporary physical fulfillment. And there haven't been any since I met you."

Anne let a derisive sound escape from her lips. "What's one more conquest?" she said.

Tears had welled up in her eyes. "Though I suppose you could congratulate yourself after this one. I *am* innocent! And I'm wearing another man's ring. You could really brag about that, couldn't you? A stupid, mixed-up, miserable little fool . . ."

"Stop that!" Evan yelled. "Damn you, you and your constant vacillation, your constant soul-searching! You know you're not in love with Larry. You know you're . . ." Evan stopped. He leaned down, at the same time reaching out to seize both of Anne's wrists in a fierce grasp, yanking her forward. His lips closed over hers, hard, hungry and unrelenting. She was so surprised by the sudden move that she could not have resisted him even if she had been able to move her arms. The pressure of his mouth was bruising and painful; her wrists felt as though they had been clamped in a vise. Yet, when the kiss had gone on for a long time, insistent and demanding, Anne felt herself melting like warm wax. A shudder ran through her, a shudder of pure ecstacy.

When he let her go, sitting back and glaring at her with a totally unexpected anger, considering the passion of his embrace, Anne was gasping for breath. "You . . . you hurt me!" she moaned. She was rubbing one wrist and then the other with her hands.

"What do you think you're doing to me?" Evan said in an accusing tone. His dark eyes flashed from her bare legs to her eyes, scanning the length of her body and bringing a rush of heat to her face. "Maybe Inez is right. Maybe you do like to see how many men you can turn on, even when you don't want them."

Anne's eyes widened. "She told you that?"

"Not in those words," Evan said. "But she told me about your provocative little bikini parade in front of that . . . that blubbery play-boy. And the result."

Evan's scathing tone was infuriating. "I was getting some sun by the pool! I didn't even know Warren was at home. You . . . you'll believe anything about me, won't you? Even when it comes from a genuine man-hunter who's so obvious . . . so insane about you . . . that . . ." Anne couldn't go on. "Take me back, please. If I didn't know it before, you've just told me why you asked me here today. You thought I was cheap and easy game. And I'm not! I don't know what it is about you . . . what's wrong with me . . . but I'm not!" Tears overcame her. Anne covered her face with her hands and let the sobs come.

Evan let her cry for a few moments before he touched her shoulder gently. "Anne?" His voice was as tender as his touch. "Anne? I'm sorry. I don't know what made me say that. I was angry and I had to strike back." His hand caressed Anne's shoulder. "It's just that I need you so much . . . ."

Anne shook her head, sobs still raking her.

"I know. You're all torn up between loyalty and your instincts. And I've just made things worse with my damned accusations. Please, won't you accept my apology?" Did he hesitate for such a long time because he found apologizing to her so difficult? Another few seconds elapsed, with no sound except that of Anne's choking sobs. Then, in a tone that was filled with the strength of conviction, Evan said, "I know you're not the kind of girl who indulges in casual affairs."

Anne gulped a deep breath of air and swiped at her eyes with the back of her wrist. "Saying you're sorry doesn't mean much when . . . when you were willing to believe I . . . oh, that horrible person!"

"I didn't believe you were out to entice Warren Delon," Evan argued quietly. "I told Inez she was a fool to think that and that she knew better herself. She's jealous of you, Anne."

Anne couldn't keep the tart sarcasm out of her voice. "Of course. You can't imagine a woman not being in love with you. Or even stand the thought."

"Now you're being unjust," Evan said. "No, I didn't believe *that*. But I was ready to leap over the wall, come over and smash Warren's face. I didn't, because I knew you wouldn't appreciate my interference. And I had no right to be jealous."

"Jealous of *Warren*?" Anne had stopped crying. Now she was tempted to laugh. "Evan, you can't be serious."

"What got me was the fact that you didn't mention the incident to me. And that you're still in that house, keeping it a secret, afraid to make waves. That's it, isn't it? If you told Mrs. Delon or Warren's wife what happened, there'd be a big blowup. Maybe put an end to your wedding plans."

"Larry would understand," Anne said. "He knows me. I imagine he knows his brother pretty well, too."

"I don't give a damn about Larry, or what he knows or what he thinks!" Evan had stopped being gentle. He was roaring at her now, his handsome face lined with fury. "It's you I'm thinking about. Why you tolerate what those people are doing to you. You're an emotional basket case, Anne. You can't think clearly enough to know what you want, what you feel."

Anne had gotten herself together enough to speak in an unemotional tone. "I told you last night that I need time to think. If you really care about me, Evan, you'll give me that time."

"I said that I need you, Anne."

She nodded. "I find that . . . hard to believe. So many women . . ."

"Believe it," Evan said firmly. "It's true. And I understand your confusion. I've been impatient because I want you so much, but I'm not an insensitive boor." Evan patted Anne's wet cheek. Then his perfect features lighted up with a smile. "Can we start all over? With my promise that I won't pressure you, I won't do anything you don't want me to do as long as you're wearing . . . *that?*" He indicated the diamond on Anne's finger with a nod of his head.

She wanted to believe him. He had said that he needed her, and more than anything else in the world, Anne wanted to believe him. She didn't have to tell Evan that what she felt for him went beyond need, was an excruciating, constant ache that might be love. As he looked into her eyes, his gaze probing and filled with emotion, she knew that he didn't have to be told. She was certain that her intense feelings were visible in her eyes. "Let me think," was all she could say. And then, suddenly aware of how she must look with her face smudged by tears, her hair a disheveled mop, she let out a little embarrassed laugh. "Don't look at me so closely. I'm a . . . I'm a mess."

"The most beautiful mess I've ever wanted to kiss," Evan said. "And I want you to know I'm going to keep my promise, dear lady. But it isn't going to be easy."

They were friends again as they sailed back to port. The electricity that Anne had felt darting between them this morning still remained, but there was less suspense. He had said that he needed her, and she had admitted to a turmoil of conflicting emotions. What she had not admitted was her fear that Evan could not be telling the truth because he was much too good for her, too exciting to be true.

When they parted on the Delons' driveway, Evan might have been her brother. "Lesson Two tomorrow?"

"Don't you have to work?"

"I'll work tonight. When I'm not thinking about . . . other things."

They both were able to laugh, a private, secret, jealously guarded laugh that only the two of them could understand. It was, Anne thought later, the kind of laughter that is shared by lovers, delightful because it closes out everyone else in the world.

Chapter Eight

During the week that followed, Anne's life seemed to be divided between two worlds. One was a storybook world in which Evan Forrester, determined to make her an expert sailor, kept his distance but told her repeatedly with his eyes and with his words that she was precious to him, that he could not even imagine a future that did not include her. Latent sexuality crackled between them like heat lightning, like a fire that was only barely under control, a thirst that was unquenched and unquenchable.

Anne's other world, also kept under control by only the most rigid emotional discipline, revolved around telephone calls from the man she had promised to marry. Each time she put down the receiver, Anne was consumed by guilt. Larry talked enthusiastically about their honeymoon, the life they would share, of his admiration for Anne's "freshness and honesty." Honesty! How could she tell him that she had not spent the day locked in Evan Forrester's arms only because Evan had made a reluctant promise and her own conscience would not allow it?

At times, talking with Larry, she felt as though she were conversing with a polite stranger. How little they knew about each other, how far apart their worlds really were! Yet she had been awed by his proposal of marriage. And he was so pleased to know that he would always be able to indulge her every whim, love her and make her happy. It seemed that Larry's long years of hard work in keeping up the family's interests had left him too little time for any but the most superficial pleasures. He had observed the family tradition at charity balls and opera openings and elegant parties, but when had he really enjoyed life the way Evan enjoyed it? Even the luxurious sports that were also a part of the Delon image were not really important to Larry. During his stay on Maui, he had never taken her out for that promised sail aboard the family's yacht. Perhaps it was an old toy, necessary for prestige, in which his interest had waned. "They rarely move that tub out of the bay," Evan had said derisively one morning as they had sailed past the yacht whose name incorporated the initials of Delon and Withrow. "A yacht's only a status symbol if you don't use it."

Anne's thoughts revolved like the pieces in a blinding kaleidescope. Give up this solid, dependable man who loved her and guaranteed an enjoyable life? Hurt and embarrass him at this stage? For what? For whom? A devastatingly handsome, sometimes erratic, always passionate man whose very glance set her on fire, whose kiss brought a rapture Larry could never evoke in her. But a man she was not sure she could trust. Evan had promised her nothing. He had said that he wanted her, and needed her. But after she had given herself to him, then what? There were all those other women who would be dazzled by his rugged masculinity, his charm, his almost indescribably good looks. If she admitted that she loved him she would pay for Larry's injured pride with her own heartbreak.

Vacillating, bewildered, Anne seemed incapable of making a decision. She kept up the facade of being Mrs. Delon's future daughter-in-law. She avoided Warren, making certain that she was never left alone with him, though his leering glances did not escape her. Nor did his sly insinuations.

Late one afternoon, after Anne had returned from her sailing lesson, Mrs. Delon, Veronica, Warren, and Inez were all sipping predinner cocktails on the lanai, the conversation desultory and, to Anne, boring.

"Well, I've had my share of engravers and calligraphers," Mrs. Delon said. She looked elegant in a mauve silk pants suit which she had accessorized with unique jewelry purchased during a Mediterranean cruise. "Shall we all drink a toast to that? The invitations will be ready to mail in exactly three days."

Everyone congratulated her on a superb

effort. She had, after all, been given so little time for the "monstrously important task." Then, dutifully, everyone drank to her accomplishment. Anne sipped from her mai tai, feeling completely left out of her own wedding plans. And she despised herself the way Evan must be despising her, because she did not lash out and cry, "But it's *my* wedding you're talking about. It's *my* life!"

Nor did she express herself honestly when Mrs. Delon announced that her favorite designer, whose last name was so well known that he didn't have to bother with his first, and about whom Anne had acquainted herself through reading fashion magazines, was going to fly to Maui to get Anne's measurements and those of members of her bridal party who were in residence. Veronica, of course, was going to be the matron of honor. And Inez Carruthers, whose mother was Mrs. Delon's best friend, was going to be one of the bridesmaids.

Anne didn't fail to see Inez's expression. The sultry blonde looking up at the ceiling with a look of stoic endurance. Veronica, as usual, smiled and said, "LeCaille wouldn't come all the way out here, personally, for anyone else but you, Mother D."

"I'll have to tolerate him somehow," Mrs. Delon sighed. "I get so weary, hearing him tell me how I ought to dress my age. He'd have me in chic little Mother Hubbards if he had his way."

There were assurances from Veronica and

Inez that Mrs. Delon didn't even begin to look
her age. The expected compliments were
smilingly acknowledged before Anne learned
that the garden wedding was going to be
staged amidst thousands of white orchids,
more than all the islands put together had
ever seen in one place. A mammoth tent
would cover the tennis court: it was being
flown in from Los Angeles. And, of course, it
was required that the gourmet food for the
reception also be flown in. Beluga caviar,
lobster, a champagne that would be acceptable were not to be purchased on a small resort
island—at least not for close to four hundred
guests.

It was all an extravagant, ostentatious
farce, Anne thought miserably. Surely Larry
couldn't know how contrived it all was, how
artificial. But then, he had business and social considerations to take into account. He
couldn't simply be indulging his mother's pen-
chant for producing spectacular parties.

Ironically, although there was no doubt that
she had thrown herself into the effort, Mrs.
Delon had yet to give any indication of affec-
tion for Anne. Her disapproval had never been
stated; it was only sensed. Was she accepting
the marriage because she knew that Larry
would not have it otherwise? Anne tried to
project herself forward to a time when she
and Larry would be alone together. She could
tolerate all this. The Delon clan would not,
after all, be accompanying the bride and

groom on their honeymoon or to their new home in Chicago.

But the thought persisted: Mrs. Delon's choice for her son would have been her dearest friend's daughter. And now Anne saw Inez flinch as Mrs. Delon said, "But enough of the wedding mechanics. Did you have a lovely sail, dear?" She smiled at Anne, looking at her with more than customary interest.

"It was fun," Anne replied. "I'm learning a lot."

"I dare say," Inez said in a purring tone.

Embarrassed by her feeling of guilt, Anne said hastily, "I don't mean that I'm such an apt pupil . . ."

"It's just that Evan is such a gifted instructor." That barbed comment came from Warren, who was slouched in his chair, half smiling at the rim of his highball glass.

Did Anne only imagine the sudden tension?

"He didn't have to teach Inez," Warren went on in a lazy drone. "You could teach *him*, couldn't you, dear girl?"

He was needling Anne and Inez at the same time, sneering and yet looking gleeful as Veronica said, "Oh, Warren, really."

Mrs. Delon leaped up, remembering that tomorrow was Amalia's day off, but that she absolutely could not spare the girl, what with the party for the servants and their friends scheduled for the next day. "I must talk to her."

Mrs. Delon's exits were always the cue that

the others were excused from the family circle. They would all be having dinner together later; now, for an hour or so, they were free to do as they pleased.

Inez, who had barely spoken to Anne in days, said that she was going to a party at one of the hotels and had better decide what she was going to wear. "If I wear my new strapless, Veronica, could I possibly borrow your fishnet shawl . . . that lovely thing with the long fringe?"

It was an almost deliberate attempt to get Veronica out of the room, and it succeeded. "Of course," Veronica said. Before Anne could get up out of her chair, Veronica had excused herself to follow Inez toward the stairway.

Warren had gotten to his feet, but now he sat down again. It would have been too obvious if Anne had fled inside. She finished her drink and set the glass down on a table. She was, after all, quite safe from his advances out here in plain view of everyone in the house.

But she was not safe, she learned a few seconds later, from Warren's nasty comments. "Alone with you at last," he said in a mocking voice. "Don't fret. Your virtue is not threatened, honey. I was raised to observe decorum at all costs."

"I wish you'd stop that," Anne said irritably.

"You can't deny that you've been avoiding me."

"I won't," Anne told him bluntly. "I have

been avoiding you. And you've made staying here very uncomfortable for me."

"My friendliness is unappreciated," Warren said with a fake sigh. "But then, one can only handle so much 'friendliness' and you seem to be getting more than your share from the neighbors."

Anne jumped up. "I don't like the things you say. I don't like the way you look at me. I don't like you, period!"

He made a chuckling sound. Did he glory in his repulsiveness? "I should think you'd be flattered to have such a plethora of male attention."

Anne's nerves snapped. "Leave me alone! Please leave me alone!" She started for the sliding glass doors. "If you don't, I . . ."

"You'll what?" Warren drawled. "Report my unseemly behavior to Mother? To Lawrence?" Just the way he pronounced his brother's name made it clear that he was jealous of his more attractive, more successful brother and detested him. Anne had stopped in her tracks, breathing hard in silent fury. "Not likely," he went on. "You have a good thing going. I might even say two. Not bad for a minor office functionary from the . . . what is the quaint way they used to put it? From the wrong side of the tracks." Warren laughed softly. "One thing we Delons have in common. We detest scenes. You wouldn't want to jeopardize your good fortune by creating a less than familial atmosphere, would you?"

"Don't tempt me," Anne warned him. She had taken all she intended to take from this disgusting lush. "Don't tempt me!" she repeated.

She was striding through the house, feeling like a fire-breathing dragon, when she nearly collided with Veronica. "Oh . . . I'm sorry. I thought you were . . ." She hadn't done anything wrong; why did she sound guilt-racked? "You were going upstairs with Inez."

"I told her where to find my shawl," Veronica said. She examined Anne's face closely, frowning. "Is something wrong?"

"No. Not a thing in the world," Anne assured her.

Veronica stared at her for a seemingly endless second. "Let's talk," she said in a low voice. "In your room, where we won't be disturbed."

What now? Anne wondered. She didn't have to wonder long. Veronica closed the bedroom door after them and turned the lock, then dropped to the edge of Anne's bed. Anne sank into one of the wicker chairs, expecting a critical lecture. What she got was a weary, hopelessly resigned, "He's been bothering you, hasn't he?"

"Who?" Anne avoided Veronica's eyes.

"Oh, you don't have to pretend with me," Veronica said. "Anne, there's nothing about this household that you can tell me. Nothing about Millicent Delon or my husband . . . not even about Larry. Do you think I don't know that Warren takes a sadistic delight in making you miserable?"

Anne lowered her head. "I'm sorry I . . . lied to you, Veronica. You don't deserve that. You're the one person here who . . ." She was going to be crying again in another instant. Anne braced herself. "I'm really sorry."

"You don't have to apologize." Her hazel eyes looked blank, as though Veronica was beyond emotion. "Do you think I don't know what Warren's like around other women, especially younger, prettier women? When he's been drinking, which is just about all the time lately, all his frustrations come out. He's . . . he's got to get back at the world somehow."

"Get back? For what?" Anne had answered her own question a few minutes ago, but she asked it anyway.

"For what's been done to him. For what he's done to himself," Veronica said. She was staring at her hands now, twisting her wedding ring around nervously. "And please don't tell me he's had everything going for him. Maybe he's had too much." Veronica closed her eyes for a moment. "Too much money and too much . . . mommy." She looked up at Anne. "I never thought I'd trust anybody enough to say that."

Anne thanked her solemnly. She couldn't resist asking, "Why do you put up with it? You must love Warren. You must have loved him to marry him . . ." Anne cut her own sentence short.

"Maybe I did, once," Veronica said. "Maybe I still do. Or maybe I just feel sorry for him. Sounds crazy, doesn't it? All this . . . not knowing how you really feel, let alone how you felt a long time ago. It's even possible that I only thought I loved Warren before . . . the wedding plans were in motion and it was too late to turn back."

They were looking directly at each other, speaking volumes without communicating in words. Is she talking about me? Anne wondered. Yes. Yes, of course she was. And Veronica was unable to explain why she tolerated her dismal situation. Maybe, after a long time, you got accustomed to it. Maybe—if you lacked the courage and the fire to assert yourself.

Veronica may have guessed her thoughts. "You're different," she told Anne. "It won't happen to you. And anyway, if you go through with it, Larry's a much more substantial human being, a totally different type."

What Veronica was saying made sense. But there was one sentence that had jarred Anne, so that she was barely listening to Veronica's other words. "You said . . . Veronica, you said, *if* I go through with it. *If*. The wedding invitations will be in the mail a few days from now. How can you doubt that . . . what makes you think . . . ?"

"Forgive me for saying this, Anne." Veronica got up from the bed and crossed the room, staring out the window toward Evan's house as she said, "There's a look. There's a . . . a feeling, something you can almost touch. When he walks up the driveway, when you see his car coming to pick you up in the morning. Or, a few days ago, when Guadelupe said he was on the phone. Remember when he called you to say he'd be a little late? You just seem to—I don't know how to describe the look. You glow. The way every woman glows when she sees or just hears the name of a man she loves."

Anne's heart had started pounding. Was it that obvious? If Veronica saw it, did the others see it, too? Warren. Yes, Warren, too. And Mrs. Delon, who made it her business to know everything that went on under her roof? If she knew, why was she so casual about the long hours Anne was spending alone with Evan Forrester?

She was stunned, but Anne tried to cover her embarrassment by saying, "You haven't mentioned a name, Veronica."

Veronica didn't turn from the window. Apparently she was embarrassed, too, at having brought up a touchy subject. "Do I have to mention a name?" She turned suddenly, her long pony-tailed hair swinging in a wide arc. Facing Anne squarely, she raised her voice above the cautious tone she had been using. "We're grown women. We're in this boat together. I thought we were talking to each other as friends." Hazel eyes bored into Anne's. "Do I really have to mention a name?"

Anne neither admitted nor denied. She was

too unsure of her own feelings to commit herself. For all she knew, Mrs. Delon had prompted this conversation, though the thought seemed unfair to Veronica, who was obviously distressed and was only trying to put out a warning signal. "I'll have to stop seeing Evan," Anne said.

"If you're not already in love with him, yes. Yes, I'd quit seeing him." Veronica walked toward the bedroom door. "It would be very easy to fall in love with him," she said in a far-away tone that startled Anne. "You wouldn't be the first resident here who did." She didn't say "house guest," as she would have had she been referring to Inez Carruthers. *Resident*. Veronica had said, "Resident." She turned back from the closed door. "It could become terribly painful, Anne. I doubt he's ever met a woman who didn't want him. I've seen him with so many, and none of them lasted very long. My impression is that he cares very much about you, but he's so . . . so charming and persuasive and sexy. He can make any woman think she's important to him."

Anne had the impression that Veronica was barely aware of another person in the room. She looked away from Anne, talking as though to herself. My God, Anne thought. Living with a domineering mother-in-law and an effete husband who seemed to prefer other female company, how easy it would be for someone as weak as Veronica to find her romantic outlet in impossible daydreams!

Was she really in love with Evan? If so, she had managed to disguise that fact more skillfully than Anne had.

Anne followed her to the door. Because it had been humiliating enough for Veronica to admit that her husband was not to be trusted, it would be cruel to hurt her even more by recognizing her symptoms of unrequited love. Anne pretended ignorance of what had just been said. She turned the subject back to herself. "If you've sensed a . . . a rapport between myself and Evan, Mrs. Delon must see it, too. I'm not admitting it's so, but . . . why would she encourage my being with Evan? She practically arranged the lessons he's been giving me on his sloop."

Veronica's face became a taut mask. "You'll have to ask that question of her," she said tersely. She was suddenly flustered, too edgy to go on. "It's getting late. I'll let you go. We'll tidy up for . . . for dinner."

"Yes," Anne said. "Thank you for talking with me. I hope you know that I want to be your friend."

"I'd like that," Veronica said. Then she unlocked the door, keeping her back toward Anne. "I'd like to be big enough to think that we can be friends." She sounded suddenly strident, then her voice turned quavery. "I think a lot of Larry and I like you . . ." Veronica left the sentence hanging in the air.

"But?"

"But there'd be a strain. I'd always keep remembering what it was like before you came here." She made a little choking sound and pulled the door open. "It wasn't paradise, but . . . it was a whole lot better before you got here. That's a terrible thing to say, but I can't help myself!" She was out of the room, her face still averted from Anne, hurrying down the hall to the room she shared with her husband before Anne could say another word.

Anne stood in the open doorway, her mouth agape, for a few seconds. Then she closed the door, crossed the room and sank to the edge of the bed where Veronica had been sitting. It was too much. Mrs. Delon, Warren, Inez, and now the one person she liked, the one who had seemed to like her and probably still did. Too much!

Anne thought about phoning Larry, about leaving the house, about going somewhere where she could be alone. Running, every possibility that occurred to her involved running.

And much later, after sitting through the brittle conversation at the dinner table, where everyone pretended that this was one big happy family, Anne walked out to the garden alone and sat on the stone bench near the wall that separated her from Evan's house. A strong breeze was whipping the palm fronds, and the music that came from Evan's office hideaway was only dimly heard. But he was up in that room, she knew, working. Working? Or thinking about her as she was thinking about him?

Then, after listening to the recorded symphony for an interminable time, Anne fought down the urges that were sweeping over her. Now there was more than one reason why she didn't want to be like Veronica. If Larry were here, dependable, thoughtful, adoring Larry, she wouldn't be confused or depressed. Tomorrow she would call him. Tomorrow everything would be all right. She glanced back at the volcanic rock wall, seeing it now as a symbol, although, Anne thought, there was more than an expanse of lava stone that separated her from Evan Forrester. There was a promise she had made to a man she could trust, a man who had placed a ring on her finger when he had declared his love.

Chapter Nine

A nother week, darling. No longer, I promise," Larry had said during his telephone call the afternoon before.

That day had passed uneventfully, even pleasantly, with the celebration of the maid's birthday. Mrs. Delon had made it a point to disappear after condescending to meet her maid's friends, leaving Anne and Veronica to supervise the festivities. With Warren out of the house, it was a relaxed and interesting occasion during which Anne almost forgot about her dilemma. Larry was coming back to Maui soon; she had to put Evan out of her mind and concentrate on her happy future as Larry's wife.

For Anne, the next day was less promising. Mrs. Delon flitted off to keep a hairdresser's appointment and to visit with friends. Veronica had looked puffy-eyed at breakfast and, complaining of a headache, had gone back to sleep, leaving her husband at the bar. Warren had started drinking earlier than usual and gave no signs of leaving the house. Anne decided that it was a good time to get away by herself to try to regenerate some enthusiasm for her forthcoming wedding.

By eleven o'clock Anne had pulled into the parking area next to the remote beach she had visited once before . . . with Evan. She crossed the sand, noting the beautiful bronze Hawaiian children playing in the tide pools a few hundred feet down the strand and the two surfers bobbing in the water, indolently waiting for a wave in a placid ocean that promised them little action. Slipping out of a short batik print kimono, Anne rubbed her face, arms, and legs with suntan oil, made herself comfortable on a huge beach towel and opened a paperback romance that she had brought along.

She was absorbed in the story for a while, but then her thoughts drifted. Why couldn't she relax and enjoy the sun the way other people here seemed to do? She felt tense, even irritable. Finally, she closed the book and returned it to her straw bag, lying back with her eyes closed against the sun's glare. Larry. She deliberately forced herself to think about Larry and how fortunate she was to have him love her, want to marry her, be so concerned about her.

Yet it was not Larry she was thinking about when she heard the sound of someone coming across the powder-fine sand toward her. Anne opened her eyes and glanced up, expecting to see the children. She gasped with surprise to see Evan standing over her, looking more than ever like a Grecian god in nothing but brief swim trunks. Anne could only stare at him, speechless.

"Hullo. Don't people say 'hi' to each other anymore?" Evan was not smiling. He sounded genuinely critical.

"Oh . . . hi. You . . . surprised me."

"Did I really?" Evan dropped to the sand next to Anne's beach towel. "I thought I told you that I come here often. And when I saw the Porsche, I said to myself, 'Well! Anne's here to see me!' Right?"

Anne sat up, conscious again of her skimpy attire. "Wrong. I came here for the same reason you told me you come here. To be alone."

Evan flashed her a dubious half-smile. "I'm being told to leave?"

He had a gift for making her feel flustered. "I didn't say that. I just . . . wanted you to know that I . . . hadn't planned a . . . planned a . . ."

"I think the word is 'rendezvous,'" Evan said. "Or would you prefer 'tryst'? Is that what you've been reading about?"

Evan gestured toward the book which had slipped out of the beach bag enough so that its romantic title was visible. Anne felt herself blushing. "You can make fun of me if you want to. You've already ridiculed my fiancé, his family and my mercenary motives in getting married." She was more comfortable now that she felt angry. "I enjoy reading about people who . . . care for each other."

"*Love* each other," Evan corrected. "You seem ill at ease with the word, Anne. Love. People who are in *love*." His dark eyes locked with Anne's, smoldering and accusing. "No, no, don't look away. Keep looking at me."

Anne let him explore her eyes for a few seconds, then found it impossible to meet his gaze. Her breath had become rapid. Her sudden excitement must be audible and visible to Evan. How he delighted in stirring emotions she didn't want stirred. What satisfaction he must derive from knowing he had this power to arouse her! As she turned away from Evan's stare, she caught a glimpse of his magnificent body, now outstretched on the sand that was as golden as his skin. Another rush of blood heated her face. "I . . . have no reason to keep looking at you," Anne said tersely.

"Except that you made me a promise," Evan reminded her. "You were going to do some serious thinking and important deciding."

Anne shuddered, her body reacting involuntarily. "Evan, I . . . I don't . . . I wish you wouldn't . . ."

"You want more time? How much time, Anne? Are you going to wait until the night before the Delons hold their big, ostentatious shindig?"

She couldn't reply. She couldn't look at him

or answer his facetious question or even explain to him that she *had* made a decision. Nor could she tell him that her decision excluded all thoughts of him.

Evan was silent for a few moments and then he said, so casually that Anne could hardly believe that a few seconds ago he had been applying a torturous flame to her heart, "I only had a cup of tea for breakfast and I'm starving. Would you like to join me for lunch?"

She knew she ought to tell Evan, sensibly, that she had come here to be alone, that she had no intention of going out on a daytime date with a man who was not her future husband and that, furthermore, she had been served a sumptuous breakfast only a few hours ago. She knew exactly what she *should* say. But what Anne said was, "What . . . did you have in mind?"

Evan laughed. "I'm not allowed to talk about what I have in mind. But I know where we can have some of the freshest mahi-mahi you've ever tasted. Sound good?"

Anne looked over to see a boyish grin on his perfect face. "I've never tasted mahi-mahi."

"Shame on the Delons' cook. It's the best fish caught around these islands. Let's go and I'll prove it to you."

Anne indicated her kimono. "I couldn't go into a restaurant wearing this."

Evan's eyes swept over her bikini. "You could go into any restaurant on the island wearing *that*," he said. "And look great. But where we're going you'll be very appropriately dressed."

He changed like the wind, Anne thought. From broodingly sexy to childishly playful. And he knew how to change her moods as readily. She felt a sense of danger in recognizing Evan's power over her. Minutes later, walking to her car, she wondered how and why he had changed her entire plan for the day. And not long after that, Anne discovered that the promised lunch was not to be served in a restaurant at all, but aboard Evan's yacht.

"We're taking a launch to lunch," he quipped as he rowed them out from the busy harbor to the magnificent white vessel that lay close to the Delons' yacht.

Anne said little on the way. She was conscious of Evan's occasional glances at her bare legs, glad that they were no longer what he called "newly arrived tourist white," and then, in the next instant, wondered why she was giving any thought to the matter at all. Hadn't she decided to put Evan out of her mind? What if she was seen with him now, going out to a boat so large that she could hardly use "sailing lessons" as her excuse to be with him?

She had another disturbing thought as Evan helped Anne aboard his yacht; she was torn between two conflicting desires. On the one hand, she dreaded the possibility that she would be alone with him, unable to trust herself, not sure of what she would do if Evan forgot their agreement and reached out for her. But on the other hand, part of her wanted him to do exactly that. Looking at his face, his strong chin and sensuous mouth, she recalled the excitement and pleasure of his lips pressed firmly against her own. Would she be able to resist him if he took her into his arms? Larry was only a dim memory when she sat this close to Evan, almost feeling the warmth of his body and certainly feeling the male magnetism that drew her closer to him, closer to wanting him.

Anne felt a pang of disappointment as she heard Evan shout, "Ahoy!" Evidently they were not going to have the yacht to themselves.

Evan's call brought two young men to the rail. They returned Evan's greeting, smiling, obviously happy to see him. In cutoff jeans and T shirts, they were typical of the healthy, sun-tanned young men who often deserted the mainland for Maui's ideal surfing and sailing. As Anne was being helped aboard, they were joined by a third crew member, this one bare-chested and bearded. They were introduced as Jim, Gary, and Craig. Anne responded to their "welcome aboards" with a smile, somewhat taken aback by the fact that none of them seemed surprised to see their employer arriving with a lone female passenger. It disturbed her to think that this was a usual occurrence,

a part of Evan's practiced routine. She wondered if Evan had let them know that he
would be arriving, if his young crew would
discreetly disappear once lunch had been
served.

There was conversation about a caulking
job that needed to be done as Anne was taken
on a tour of the yacht, and all three of the
young men took turns with Evan in pointing
out the solid brass fixtures, the teak decking,
the beautifully appointed cabin spaces and
the gleaming stainless-steel galley. They appeared to be as proud of the yacht as its owner
and as comfortable with him as though he
were just another member of the crew.

How could so much fun be mingled with
such strange, aching disappointment? Anne
was pressed into service as the salad maker
while Evan and Gary prepared the freshly
caught mahi-mahi and Craig mixed his spe-
cialty, "man-sized mai tais that don't taste
like the punch at a little kids' party." They
carried their plates and drinks to an um-
brella-shaded table on the aft deck, the others joining Evan and Anne as easily as if
they were expected to. No, Anne decided, they
had not been warned that their skipper was
bringing a lady friend aboard. Evan's meeting
with her on the beach had been unplanned
and his crew members knew that they were
not obliged to clear the decks.

They played poker after the table had been
cleared, and it was Gary who suggested after

an hour or so that they all take a dip. Swimming over the side was pleasant, but Evan kept his distance. There were no accidental brushes against her body, no attempts to touch her. And when it was time to go back aboard, it was Craig who boosted Anne up out of the water and Jim who gave her his hand and pulled her up on deck.

As the afternoon lazed on, Anne sunned herself in one of the canvas lounge chairs while Evan busied himself below, listening to an idea Gary had come up with that would improve reception on the ship-to-shore radio. Evan was a casual and gracious host, but nothing more. If he was deliberately playing hard to get, aware of his powerful attraction, he was doing a superb job of it. She had all she could do not to stare at the magnificence of his tall, beautifully proportioned frame as he came back on deck, still clad only in his swimming trunks, still acting as though he had never swept Anne into a passionate embrace or invited her to come aboard this luxurious ship when their privacy would have been assured.

Damn him! He was purposely teasing her, lowering his warm, sun-bronzed body onto the deck just beside her chair, so close that the enticing male scent of him alerted her to his nearness even with her eyes closed.

"Enjoying yourself?" he queried in his deep lazy voice.

"Mmm," she responded, hoping her murmured reply would not betray the quick surge of excitement his presence provoked. It was impossible to put her feelings on ice as Evan seemed so easily to do.

"I thought you might be getting thirsty," he remarked, "so I had Craig mix us a couple more mai tais." Anne opened her eyes and noticed for the first time the tray which he'd brought up from the galley to place beside her on the gleaming teak deck. Two tall frosty glasses sat on it, and suddenly Anne was aware of just how parched her throat had become in the blazing afternoon sun. Here was one desire which could be satisfied easily enough, she thought wryly, reaching out for the ice-cold drink. But Evan's hand was there before hers, sending an electric tingle through her as their fingers met and he handed her the drink. His black eyes laughingly acknowledged her response.

"Thank you," she murmured, blushing.

"A loving cup," he smiled, taking a sip of his own drink. "It's funny the way you sometimes don't realize how much you want something until it's sitting right in front of you." The teasing look in his eyes left no doubt as to his meaning. And she had to admit that his lean, tanned body lounging completely at ease on the deck at her feet was something she did want, very much.

"Yes, but sometimes one longs for what's faraway and out of reach," she parried.

"You know what they say—out of sight, out

of mind. I'd be more tempted by something I could get my hands on." Anne felt a delicious shiver run through her as he trailed his fingers, still cool from holding his frosty drink, along her slim golden leg. His light caress started at her instep and traveled slowly, maddeningly up her calf to linger on the sensitive skin behind one knee. He traced patterns of delight across her smooth thigh, his cool touch incongruously creating a languorous warmth somewhere deep inside her.

"Evan," she protested, placing her hand over his to stop its persistent ascent, "you promised . . ."

"That I wouldn't do anything you don't want me to do. But you want this, Anne . . . as much as I do." His coal-black eyes fixed hers in a hypnotic gaze. "Admit it," he drawled slowly, seductively, and his hand turned to catch her wrist like a gentle yet inescapable vise. "Admit that you're burning for my touch. You've been waiting for me to do this all afternoon."

She shook her head slowly in mute denial, but at the same moment he drew her from the lounge chair to the smooth hard deck beside him. She was putty in his hands, her will having seemed to desert her as his arms closed around her and a wave of sweet abandon left her too dizzy to protest.

One hand slid down over her hips to press her sun-warmed body close against his muscular thighs, to mold her softness to his hard masculine frame. Evan cradled her head in the crook of his arm and gazed down at her with sensuous longing until she felt she would drown in the deep black pools of his eyes.

"You want me to make love to you," he whispered with compelling certainty. With a little moan she arched her body into his, unconsciously inciting his answering thrust. Her lips parted under the thrilling seduction of his kiss.

After that one, endless moment of waiting, when her whole life seemed poised on the brink of some momentous discovery, she gave herself up to him willingly. They clung to each other wildly, each caught up in the whirling vortex of their mutual desire. His body seemed a magnet which pulled at her center, sending waves of ecstasy coursing through her as he surged against her thighs, forcing a recognition of his manhood.

Somehow, her bikini top was no longer properly fastened and Evan's hands were moving softly, agonizingly over her rounded breasts. Each tantalizing caress seemed to drive her onward toward some new peak of pleasure that heretofore had only been vaguely dreamed of. His warm hard mouth trailed kisses of fire down her throat, urging her to do his bidding, to arch still closer to him. When his lips closed over one highly sensitized tip she moaned with a desire she could no longer contain.

The sound of her voice hoarsely repeating his name was suddenly drowned out by the chug-chugging of a motor starting up.

"What the . . . ?" Evan's voice was harsh as he momentarily raised his head, then swiftly got to his feet to stride angrily to the side of the boat. Dazed and more than a little embarrassed, Anne groped for her bikini top and refastened the tie. By the time Evan turned from the railing with a wry look on his face, she was taking a nervous sip from her tall mai tai in a vain attempt to calm the furious beating of her heart.

"I guess the boys decided it was time to make themselves scarce," Evan explained with a sheepish grin. "They're really not accustomed to a show like that in the middle of the afternoon. They've taken the launch and, from the looks of it, they'll hang out on shore for a couple of hours before returning." She stared at him in disbelief for several moments.

"No doubt that's all part of the routine when your lady friends come calling," Anne finally managed to bite out, appalled at what she had almost allowed to happen. And she had thought he was sticking to his word when she saw the three crew members on board!

"Now wait a minute. I had nothing to do with . . ."

"I think you'd better take me home, Evan,"

Anne interrupted stiffly, and she refused to listen to another word he had to say.

The ride in to shore was a silent one and the sun was just beginning to set as Evan escorted her with formal determination back to the white Porsche. As he helped her into the driver's seat, Evan's hand touched Anne's elbow in a gesture of apology. "Please, Anne. Let me explain. I know you're upset by all this," he commented as Anne settled herself behind the wheel.

"What makes you say that?" she retorted sarcastically.

"You're shaking."

Evan was right, but she was not about to admit it. Anne made a useless attempt to calm herself. It was impossible to stop the quavering sensation inside her. Nor could she give him a face-saving excuse for the way her hands shook on the steering wheel. He knew only too well what was causing it.

"Are you queasy about going back and explaining where you've been? I won't tell if you won't, but I hate sneaking around, don't you?"

Anne looked up to see an intense, somewhat derisive stare leveled at her. "I wasn't . . . 'sneaking around,' as you so charmingly put it. I'm not a . . . captive in the Delons' house." She wanted to add something about being free to do as she chose, but she knew it wasn't true. What *would* she say to account for her long absence? If she told the truth, it would inevitably get back to Larry. If she lied and was caught in the lie it would be even worse. If only she were completely innocent and could face any suspicion with righteous indignation. But that was impossible now. Bitterly, she said, "It wasn't the best idea in the world, though, was it? If someone wants to make something of it, I'll be hanged for a lamb instead of a lion."

"And that's too bad. We could have given people something to really talk about if you weren't being such a hypocrite."

Anne gasped. "How can you say . . . ?"

"Because that's what you are!" Evan raged. "You can't be so confused that you don't know what you're doing . . . to me, to yourself, yes, and to the damned fool who thinks you're in love with him."

Anne's hands shot to her face, covering her eyes. "Stop that! I don't have to listen to any more of your insults!" She shuddered, took her hands away from her eyes and inserted the ignition key into the lock.

Before Anne could turn the key, Evan's hand closed over her wrist, his fingers pressing down in a powerful, viselike grip. "Don't run away! You're going to listen to me!"

Anne tried twisting her arm free of the iron grasp. "Let me go! You . . . you're hurting me!"

"Not as much as you're hurting yourself and everyone around you," Evan shouted. "You know there's an attraction between us that isn't going to go away. If you were in love with Larry Delon, it couldn't have happened. But you persist in playing your little game. I'm supposed to wait in the wings while you decide whether or not you want to go on letting the Delons stage their big wedding extravaganza. I was *told* to wait. I've been expected to behave like a eunuch, holding off while Miss Untouchable decides where she's going to get the better deal!"

Anne made a violent motion that took Evan by surprise. His hand slipped from her wrist and he made no further attempt to stop her from starting the car. As she started the motor, Anne cried, "I'm not interested in making 'deals'! You . . . you're the most hateful man I've ever known!"

"You didn't think that when I held you in my arms! You didn't think that when I kissed you!" Evan's rage blazed in his dark eyes and his face was a taut mask, marring his handsomeness. "You're nothing but a tease. And there's no more detestable woman on earth than a tease!"

"All right, we're in agreement. We can't stand the sight of each other!" Anne revved the motor, but Evan's hands clutched the top of the car door. Backing out of the parking space would have thrown him off balance. That, at least, was Anne's excuse for not roaring away from the spot. "It might interest you to know that I . . . I came to a conclusion while I was on the beach. Before you got there, I knew . . . I knew I must have been insane . . . to think I don't want to be Larry's wife. You . . . you poisoned my mind against Larry, lumping him with his family, when you know perfectly well he's not like them. He's . . . he's . . ."

"He's somebody you were able to put out of your 'poisoned mind' when I showed up on the beach this morning," Evan countered angrily. "Were you thinking about him when you agreed to come with me? Were you thinking about him when I held you in my arms?"

"I didn't know where we were going," Anne protested. The argument sounded weak and flimsy even to her own ears. "I thought . . . in a . . . public restaurant, just having lunch with . . . with a neighbor . . ."

"You'd be perfectly respectable?" Evan sneered the words. "But you didn't object when you found out where we were going. And you didn't know there'd be anyone else aboard. Did you? *Did you, Anne?*"

She knew that her face had turned scarlet. And she could think of nothing to say, no plausible explanation that she could offer him.

Evan's voice had softened, but he still sounded cuttingly sarcastic. "You came aboard with me because you want the same thing I want. You showed me that this afternoon. The only difference between us is that I'm honest enough to admit it."

Anne could only get back at him with a

caustic attempt at laughter. "You flatter yourself, Mr. Forrester. You think that because
you're some kind of . . . of sex symbol around
this island that every woman you look at is
going to fall all over you. Well, count me out.
I'm sorry I ever met you. And I'll thank you to
stay out of my life from now on." She started
to back the car, but Evan did not move. "I'd
like to go home now, if you don't mind!"

"Home. Yes, by all means home. With the
rest of those phonies. It's where you belong."
Evan straightened up, taking his hands away
from the car door. "If they ask you where you
were, tell them you spent the day with another 'great catch.' "

Anne turned to face Evan, glaring. "I'll tell
them just what I choose to tell them. It's none
of your business!"

Infuriatingly, Evan laughed as he backed
away from the car. "Yes, but what story are
you going to tell yourself? That you didn't
want my kiss? Don't try to kid yourself!"

Anne was racing the car away from the
beach parking area when Evan's shout followed her: "If I hadn't tried to seduce you,
you'd have been terribly disappointed!"

She drove like fury, the little white car
roaring toward the main road, tires shrieking
on the gravel as she made the sharp turn. He
had to be the most egotistical man on earth!
He'd known all along how she felt and he *had*
been playing hard to get, assured that his
incredible physique and handsome face and

dashing personality were having a devastating effect upon her. He'd smugly let Anne know that he was only available when *he* wanted to be, in his own good time. How did he *dare* to imply that she would have been "terribly disappointed" if he hadn't tried to make love to her?

Speeding back toward the Delon estate, Anne glanced into the rearview mirror to see if Evan's car was behind her. It wasn't. Maybe he had decided to stay at the beach. Or maybe he had gone back to the yacht. It didn't matter. All that mattered was that she had allowed him to make a fool of her. And he'd had the audacity to jeer at her. *"Terribly disappointed!"* The words stuck in Anne's consciousness like a dagger, twisting and turning, filling her with anger and humiliation. How could she have cheapened herself to this degree? How could she have lowered herself and made a pitiable laughing stock out of a fine man like Larry Delon?

Anne's questions were answered late that night. Sleepless, after an encounter with Inez Carruthers, she sat on the edge of her bed, still trembling, wishing that she could have the relief of tears. "Have a good time today?" Inez had asked. Mrs. Delon, Veronica, and Warren were all alerted by the insinuating purr Inez affected. Anne had made an embarrassed, mumbling response, knowing that Inez would not have asked the question if she had not, somehow, known how Anne had spent her day. And Inez had looked at her with a derisive, satisfied expression, saying, "I ran into Craig Chapman a while ago. We were both buying cigarettes. And he said you'd had a marvelous little lunch and poker party aboard Evan's yacht." Waiting for raised eyebrows and pregnant silences from the others, Inez had added an innocent-sounding, gratuitous explanation: "Don't panic, anybody. Evan's visits to the yacht are always chaperoned by his crew. At least they always are when I'm there." Inez's tinny laugh was obviously intended to imply that such was not the case during Anne's visit.

Mrs. Delon and Veronica heard the news without comment, but Anne noticed a coolness in their manners for the rest of the evening. Most sickening was Warren's total silence and the snide expression on his face. It was as though he were telling Anne that he had been right about her all along: she was available, and her aloofness, her rejection of him, was just a pose. An explanation would only have compounded Anne's guilty feeling. She said nothing about why she had spent the day with Evan. When she excused herself and went to her room, she felt sick with nausea.

But worse than the subtle inquisition she had undergone with the Delons and their nasty house guest was the crushing realization that what Evan had said was right. She *had* been disappointed. She *had* yearned for Evan to take her into his arms. She hated him, yet she wanted that even now. And all her promises to herself, to forget Evan and to appreciate the man she had promised to marry, floated away with the tears that finally came, the tears with which she cried herself to sleep.

Chapter Ten

𝒜nne devoted the next five days to the reason that had brought her to Maui. It was an effort to put her doubts and confusions aside, but she kept reminding herself that her approaching marriage to Larry Delon was an exciting and important event—one that any woman in her right mind would be thrilled about. Evan Forrester was a temporary abberation; it was only her lack of experience with men that had swept away her reason. His unusual charm, his expert line, and her loneliness without Larry had been a deadly combination, but that was all over now, Anne assured herself. Her telephone conversations with Larry concerned themselves with wedding plans.

"Everything going along smoothly, then?" Larry asked during one of his afternoon calls.

"Your mother sees to that," Anne told him. "She's a remarkable organizer."

"And you aren't feeling . . . left out?"

Anne hesitated. "Why would I feel that way, Larry?"

"Well, several times I . . . got the impression . . ." Larry cut himself off. "I'm glad, darling. Mother has a way of taking over, but I'm sure you understand." Larry chuckled amiably. "Her younger son has never gotten married before. It's a tremendous social responsibility. And you must admit she's admirably qualified to take it on."

Larry had sounded pleased. No mention was made of Evan; nothing was said to indicate that Mrs. Delon had talked with him privately about Anne's behavior. *Maybe I've misjudged Larry's mother,* Anne decided. *I'll try to get on better with her from now on.*

It was not easy. Mrs. Delon seemed to live in a world of her own. And if she disapproved of something or, more importantly, of someone, her comments were always casually cruel. She expressed herself in strong terms and expected to get her way in even the most minor matters. There was no hope of establishing a warm rapport with her, Anne decided after several attempts. The most one could hope for was civilized tolerance.

It was Mrs. Delon who personally met her favorite dress designer at the airport, saw that he was properly entertained, and examined his preliminary sketches with a critical eye. "You really must make more of Anne's tiny waistline," she said, nodding at Anne as though she were a store-window mannequin.

LeCaille, who answered only to his last name, was a small, nervous man with a dapper blond moustache and hands that were never still. "An excellent point, Mrs. Delon, excellent." He stared at Anne, also regarding her as an inanimate object. "I would not have believed those measurements." He busied himself, making notes on a sketch pad, nodding his approval of Mrs. Delon's comments about French lace and seed pearls, approving her aqua and apricot color scheme for the bridesmaids.

It was while Inez's measurements were being taken that Anne's discomfort became acute.

"Remarkable," the noted designer said with enthusiasm. "Your measurements have not changed a whit since I dressed you for your debut. At the time I thought I would be designing your wedding gown before too long."

Mrs. Delon and Inez exchanged quick glances. "I suppose I misunderstood your dear mother, Inez. But, I made the mistake of thinking you and the younger Mr. Delon . . ."

Mrs. Delon cleared her throat meaningfully and LeCaille looked embarrassed. "Yes, it was a silly misunderstanding on my part," he apologized.

"It's quite all right," Inez said. "It's not as though Mother and dear Mrs. Delon didn't suppose that Larry and I would be getting married one day. It's simply that he and I decided that we . . . weren't temperamentally suited to each other."

It was the first time Anne had seen Larry's mother lose control of a conversation or of her always perfect poise. She turned and flounced out of the room, her anger barely disguised. She left behind her an uneasy quiet.

"I have said something offensive," LeCaille said in a mournful tone. "But, I am an artist, not a diplomat."

"It's simply that Mrs. Delon has never gotten over her disappointment," Inez said soothingly. She favored Anne with a patronizing smile. "I think Larry's made an excellent choice, don't you? I would have made him a miserable wife. I'm a little too fond of excitement."

She was telling Anne that she had found Larry too dull for her taste. And that her fondness for "excitement" meant an interest in more dynamic men. *One dynamic man,* Anne thought, suddenly depressed. *Evan.*

As if she had looked into Anne's mind, Inez tossed her blond hair impatiently. "I have a tennis date, LeCaille. Will you need me much longer? It's only next door, but I did promise to be on the court at three."

"I did not travel all this distance to watch you play tennis," the little man said imperiously. "I do not, except for very important clients, take measurements myself. And I daresay Mrs. Delon will consider your gown of more importance than your appointment to play tennis."

Inez was chastened. Anne was excused shortly afterward and was in her room, looking out the window as Inez hurried down the driveway, dazzling in a chic white tennis dress, obviously in a hurry to keep her glee-fully announced date with Evan Forrester.

It was only because she had acted like a fool that she felt this gnawing, painful sensation. It couldn't be jealousy, Anne's mind argued. Hurt pride, perhaps, but not jealousy. Yet the hurt was very real. Anne hoped, during the days that followed, that her unreasoning re-sentment of Inez was well hidden, though, try as she would, she could not hide it from herself.

Mrs. Granger, the unsmiling, taciturn housekeeper to the Delons, was talking with Veronica one afternoon as Anne came into the solarium with a book. "Am I interrupting something?" Anne asked.

"Not at all," Veronica assured her. "Binny just came in to ask how many to expect at the dinner table tonight."

"You, Miss Beal?" the housekeeper asked. Her manner was always as proper and imper-sonal as her starched uniform.

"Yes, I'll be here," Anne told her. "I . . . don't have any plans."

Mrs. Granger nodded primly, said, "Thank you," and marched out of the sunny room.

"She's doing individual soufflés," Veronica explained. "So, of course, she wants an accu-rate head count. Not too many of us tonight." Veronica waved at a rattan armchair. "Join the party." She sounded bitter.

Anne sat down, aware that Veronica was not in a good mood. "Mrs. Delon said she was going to spend the evening with friends after she took LeCaille to the airport," she said.

"And Warren's gone. I don't expect to see him until the wee hours, if at all, tonight." Veronica made a wry face. "Par for the course." She didn't seem to be troubled by her husband's absence. But she sounded vindictive as she added, "And we won't be seeing Inez at dinner. She'd already told dear old Binny not to expect her for dinner." Veronica's lips pressed together in a hard line.

"Well, that leaves just the two of us," Anne said, trying to sound indifferent.

Veronica was not quite ready, it seemed, to close the subject there. "Yes, Evan's having some of his business associates to dinner on the yacht tonight. Inez told me yesterday that she hoped she'd be asked. It would seem that she got her wish."

There was no mistaking Veronica's jealous resentment. Anne had an urge to cry out, "This is insane. You're a married woman. I'm about to marry into this family. How can we sit here and be upset because Inez and Evan are going to be together tonight—are probably together right now? They're exactly right for each other: vain, self-centered, complementing each other's insatiable egos." Veronica lapsed into a grim, brooding silence.

Anne opened her book and tried to concentrate on the words before her. She heard Veronica suddenly push back her chair and, without another word, stamp out of the room.

Had Evan encouraged Veronica, too? Had

he given her reason to believe that he was interested in her? Probably, Anne decided. He made a game out of undermining other men and flattering women, encouraging them to draw a comparison between the men in their lives and himself. In Warren's case, the comparison had to be a foregone conclusion. But how cruel to play on the emotions of a weak, unloved, aimless woman like Veronica! The incident strengthened Anne's determination to put Evan Forrester completely out of her mind. Yet the words on the page before her blurred. She visualized Inez serving as Evan's hostess aboard the yacht—smiling, looking glamorous, charming his business associates. And afterward, when the dinner party was over, would Evan's crew again discreetly disappear in the launch, leaving him alone with Inez?

Telling herself that she didn't care didn't erase the aggravating images from Anne's thoughts. She couldn't read. She closed the book, furious with herself for having let Evan get under her skin, but the needling thoughts persisted. And it was not only her mind that plagued her. Her body yearned for Evan's embrace, even as she despised him for what he had done to her. His kisses were seared upon her lips, like fiery brands. As Veronica had done earlier, she leaped to her feet and hurried out of the room, with no special destination, as though it were possible to run away from herself and the strange sickness that had taken possession of her.

She would call Larry. The sound of his calm, controlled voice would bring her back to reality. But when she reached his office, she was told that Mr. Delon had left for the day. When she put in a call to his home, his valet reported that Mr. Delon had taken a client to dinner and was not expected home until late.

For the first time since he had left Maui, Larry did not call Anne in the evening. Yet she found herself not caring. She even hoped that his client would turn out to be an attractive female. For some inexplicable reason she would then feel less guilty for the shameful emotions that threatened to overwhelm her.

Her dinner was solitary. Veronica had pleaded another headache, Anne was told by one of the maids. Anne could barely choke down the superbly prepared dinner. How would she ever get through the long night alone? Alone with her dreams of a man who detested her, yet held her close and told her repeatedly that she was about to take a step that would forever ruin her life.

Chapter Eleven

$\int$he had slept fitfully. Anne woke to discover that it was after ten. She felt tired, her muscles aching as though she had gotten no sleep at all. And her disgust with herself brought a new determination. She had wasted enough time and energy thinking about Evan Forrester. She had let herself become so sidetracked that she barely took an interest in planning the most important event of her life.

She showered, dressed, and went downstairs determined to turn over a new leaf. She had been blaming Larry's mother for taking over her wedding plans. Maybe she was to blame. Perhaps if she had shown more interest, Mrs. Delon wouldn't have been forced to take complete charge. Today will be different, Anne thought. Today I'm going to start being as happy and excited as I was the night Larry asked me to marry him.

A long shower had erased most of the effects of her restless night. She applied her makeup carefully. Her turquoise and white striped sun dress looked fresh and almost partylike. Vigorous brushing had brought out the sun-bleached highlights in her hair. She was going to start behaving like Larry Delon's bride-to-be. Everyone, she told herself, would notice a dramatic change in her this morning.

There was no one around, Anne discovered, to notice. Guadalupe served her breakfast next to the pool, reporting, in answer to Anne's question, that only the servants were in the house, Miss Carruthers had not returned the night before. Nor had Mr. Delon. And Warren Delon's wife had gone to Kahalui with her mother-in-law to see a doctor.

Anne expressed her concern and was informed that Veronica's recurring headaches had become a source of worry with the senior Mrs. Delon. This morning, over Veronica's protests, an appointment had been made with a neurologist, who was also a friend of the family.

Anne felt let down. And the day yawned endlessly before her. Part of her problem, she realized, was having nothing constructive to do. She had worked all of her adult life. She had, in fact, rather enjoyed being productive. After she and Larry were married, although he had made it clear that the idea of her holding a job was unthinkable, she would have to find some useful way to spend her time. Strange. It was almost impossible to think of herself as the wife of an enormously wealthy man. What did the wives of rich husbands do to prevent boredom? Some sort of volunteer work, Anne thought. Yes, she

would involve herself in some charitable
cause, some project connected with the many
civic, altruistic, and cultural programs that
she knew were of interest to Larry. She was
determined not to waste her days as Veronica
did, subjecting herself to idle romantic daydreams. Perhaps there was some organic reason for Veronica's headaches, but it was more
likely that they were psychosomatic manifes-
tations of her unfulfilling life.

Unfortunately, Anne's projected visions of
being a volunteer worker in some worthy en-
deavor had nothing to do with the immediate.
This day's emptiness filled her with fear. With
nothing of significance to do, her thoughts
might drift to a subject that she had forbidden
her mind to entertain. She didn't want to start
thinking about Inez, wondering where the
Delons' other house guest had spent the night,
and with whom. She didn't want to wonder if
Evan was at home or still aboard his yacht. If
she didn't control her thoughts, she might . . .

She *was* thinking about him! Anne left most
of her breakfast untouched and returned to
her room. She got out of her sun dress and into
a Hawaiian print bikini Larry had bought for
her at Whaler's Village. Swimming would use
up her physical energy, at least. Her earlier
tiredness had been replaced by a nervous
frustration that made it impossible to sit still.
And maybe, if she swam long enough, she
would be able to relax and think more logi-
cally.

A towel flung over her shoulder, Anne was

on her way down the stairs when she heard a door slam. Seconds later, Warren Delon was lurching up the steps, meeting Anne in the middle of the stairway.

He glanced upward, his eyes bloodshot and barely open. Then, as Anne stepped aside, murmuring a startled "Hello," Warren's sensual face widened in a broad, lascivious grin. "Saw me 'rriving," he slurred. "Came to meet me. Now, that's what I call a . . . sweet, 'siderate li'l girl."

"I didn't see you," Anne protested. "If I had, I wouldn't have . . ."

"Oh, c'mon . . . c'mon. Don't le's be coy, honey!" Warren's ridiculing words were accompanied by a sudden move forward. Grasping Anne around the waist in a smothering hug, he threw her off balance. She cried out in surprise as they both nearly toppled down the stairs. Then, leaning against the solid wall of the stairwell for support, reeking of alcohol, Warren began a mindless, animal pawing of Anne's body that filled her with revulsion. She summoned a vicious burst of strength as his wet lips smashed crookedly against hers. He tumbled backward, cursing her as Anne screamed, "Get away from me, you . . . you . . ." She could think of no description vile enough to account for his outrageous handling of her body.

Anne heard him thudding against the wall, his huge arms flailing in the air. Then, with a furious bellow, Warren fell backward, landing near the foot of the stairs on his back.

Anne stood looking at him in frozen horror. What if his back were broken? What if he were dead? Her breath suspended, she started down the stairs. In almost the same instant, Mrs. Granger, Amalia and Bertram Knowles, the butler, came running to the foot of the stairs from different directions. The butler was just helping a groggy, groaning Warren to his feet as the front door opened to admit Veronica and Mrs. Delon.

Warren was apparently none for the worse for his fall. With help from the servants, he clambered to his feet, muttering incoherently. Mrs. Delon, wide-eyed, marched up to him, her voice strident. "What is going on here?" She didn't ask if her older son were hurt. Imperious, she looked from him to Anne, demanding. "Exactly what *is* going on here?"

Anne didn't wait for an unjust accusation. She still felt the rapacious grappling touch of Warren's hands. She was too incensed with him, with all of them, to care what she was saying. "He's lucky!" she cried. "He's lucky I didn't kill him! If he ever lays a hand on me again, I will! So help me, I'll kill him!"

Veronica's face was a study in pain. The servants looked embarrassed but not surprised. Even Mrs. Delon seemed to be at a loss for words.

"This isn't the first time!" Anne heard herself shouting. She felt nude and exposed, standing before them in her skimpy bathing suit, but that didn't matter anymore. "I've had it," she shouted. "I've had it with all of you! I'm supposed to be thrilled to death, staying in this house. I'm supposed to be the grateful nobody! Well, where I come from, I wouldn't have to worry about having to avoid a . . . a disgusting, drunken, lecherous *pig!*"

Warren's string of curses was hushed by his mother. "Be quiet, Warren! It may just be that you owe Anne an apology." She whirled on Bertram. "Get him to his room. See that he's not broken any bones." Mrs. Delon turned to the other servants. "I don't think you will be needed," she said in a cold, dismissing manner. The others drifted away, looking uncomfortable.

Veronica had not gone to her husband. She stood, as if in a trance, staring at him, deliberately looking away from Anne.

As Warren was led up the stairs, Anne moved aside to let him pass. Neither Warren nor the butler glanced in her direction as they moved past Anne. As they reached the top of the stairs and turned, Anne started to follow, headed for her own room. She wanted only to get out of this house and away from everyone in it. She was stopped by Mrs. Delon's voice. Hoarse, croaking, lacking her usual authoritative manner, Mrs. Delon called up to Anne, "I will see that an apology is forthcoming, Anne. I will also be very appreciative if you don't upset Lawrence with this unfortunate incident. Please let me take care of it in my own way."

Anne hesitated for an instant and then

stamped up the few remaining stairs that took her to the hallway. "I don't care what you do," she said. "I just want out!"

She reached her room, locking the door behind her. For a while, she leaned against it, trying to catch her breath, shaking with anger. No one had followed her. From down the hall, she heard Bertram saying, "Let's get you out of these clothes, sir. And I'll send for black coffee."

At least there had been no argument about what had caused the ugly scene. Mrs. Delon and Veronica must be all too familiar with Warren's behavior, especially after he had been drinking. But the promised apology didn't help. Neither did Mrs. Delon's concern that Larry would be told what had happened. Hypocritically, she would pretend that all was ideal in this marvelous household. Any tinge of scandal was unthinkable. And Veronica was even more detestable. How could she live with a man who was a known lecher? How could she look the other way? In exchange for what? A luxurious life, supervised by a domineering woman who wanted only to keep up the façade of respectability and prominence? Anne felt close to nausea.

It took another few minutes before she thought about cramming clothes into suitcases. Then, recognizing that most of her wardrobe had been paid for with Delon money, she stopped suddenly. She didn't want any reminders. She wanted to leave, go somewhere, anywhere. She wanted to erase the Delons from her mind. But she wasn't ready to pack. Where would she go?

She hadn't promised Mrs. Delon that she wouldn't call Larry. He was not at fault, and she owed him an explanation. Yet, when Anne reached for the telephone, she wondered what his reaction would be when she told him the sordid little tale. He would be appalled, of course. But would his disgust extend to her? Would he, like Veronica, remind Anne that everything had been serene in the Delon household before her arrival?

Anne turned away from the telephone. She didn't want to talk to Larry. She wanted to be alone, to cry, to think, to return to the peaceful, ordinary existence that she had lived before she had become entangled with the Delon family. And she knew, in thinking those thoughts, that it would always be the Delon *family;* Larry could not separate himself from them. Even distance would not help. In marrying him, she would be reducing herself forever to a life in which Mrs. Delon said, "Please let me take care of it in my own way."

Where could she go? And could she go back to the mainland without so much as calling Larry? Churning with mixed emotions, Anne forgot about calling the airport for a plane reservation, and changed into a simple yellow and white striped T shirt and jeans. Maybe a few hours alone somewhere would help her get her thoughts together.

She managed to get down the stairs without

encountering anyone. Once out in the parking area, she hesitated. She didn't want to drive one of the family cars. She had the keys to the Porsche in her straw handbag, but she could hardly say that she wanted no more to do with the Delons and then drive off in one of their gleaming sportscars. Resolutely, Anne started up the driveway. She would walk, she decided. Just keep walking. She'd find an access path to the beach sooner or later. Her legs had not stopped shaking; walking was a teetering effort.

Close to tears, she was on the main road, a few yards past the gateposts that defined Evan Forrester's estate, when she heard a car motor behind her. Anne stepped to the gravel shoulder, resolutely increasing her pace, looking down at the ground. A dark sedan passed her. Anne kept walking. She hadn't looked up to see the driver. Then, feeling faint from the hot sun, she slowed down and looked ahead to see that the sedan had pulled over to the edge of the road. If she didn't turn back, she would have to walk past the car.

Anne felt an inner fluttering of fear. Young women didn't go walking along these roads alone. Larry had warned her that being alone anywhere on the island was not advisable. Yet she kept moving forward, not knowing what else to do. She had never seen the dark sedan before; her first thought, that Mrs. Delon had sent one of the servants to follow her and persuade her to come back, was obviously wrong.

Anne was within a few feet of the parked car, her heart beating a rapid tattoo, when she saw the door on the driver's side open. A blackness came over her. She stopped, swaying, trying to hold onto consciousness, though she felt more faint when she stopped than when she had been walking. There was a micro instant when she saw the man who had gotten out of the sedan and then she felt her legs collapsing under her. Evan Forrester was running toward her. He was calling her name and running. Before her body dropped to the side of the road, she felt the support of two strong arms.

How much time had elapsed, Anne wondered, since she had felt herself falling into oblivion? She was lying on a king-sized bed in a room she had never seen before. Someone was stroking her forehead. Anne's eyes turned to see Evan sitting at the edge of the bed, his eyes clouded with concern. His fingers ran over her temple, the touch a gentle caress as he said, "Don't panic, Anne. You're with me. Do you want me to send for a doctor?"

Anne shook her head, dazed. "What happened? I guess I . . . I guess . . ."

"Heat prostration," Evan said evenly. "Are you sure you're all right? I shouldn't have carried you up here. I should have gotten you to a doctor in town."

Anne started to sit up in the bed, then fell back to the mound of pillows stacked behind her head. "No. No, really. I just got . . . a little dizzy. I'm fine now."

"My housekeeper's fixing an ice pack for your head. And something to drink." Evan smiled. "One of her magic Huna preparations, I imagine. What were you doing, walking along the road? Where could you possibly have been going?"

Anne thought for a moment, recalling the episode with Warren. She didn't want to talk about it, but she had gone this far. It seemed dishonest to do anything but tell Evan exactly what had happened. She gave him a sketchy review.

"That repulsive excuse for a man," Evan said, almost to himself. "But at least you let Mommy know that you've had enough. And after that, what? Where *were* you going, Anne?"

Anne shrugged, suddenly feeling lost and foolish. "I don't know where I was going, Evan. I feel like such an idiot. I was like a . . . like a stupid little kid, running away from home."

Evan's hand found hers, pressing it warmly. "I'd like to think you were coming here. But you weren't. You'd passed my driveway. Why didn't you turn in? Come to me?"

Anne pressed her eyes shut. "I didn't think you'd be home."

"Why wouldn't I be home? Well, I did have an appointment in Lahaina, but this morning I was here until . . ."

"I knew you were with Inez," Anne said tersely. "And she hadn't gotten home yet."

Evan stared at her for a long time. Then, inexplicably, he made an amused sound in his throat. "You know what? Do you know what? You just sounded the way I've been hoping you'd sound. Jealous!"

Anne bristled. "Of Inez? Of . . . her being with you? That's ridiculous!"

"It really is," Evan conceded. "Especially since I said good night to her shortly before ten last night. She didn't seem to want to leave the boat, but I'd told her I was going home to work. And there was one of my associates—Gordy Wyndham—just dying to see her home. He's getting over his third traumatic divorce and is enormously attracted to blondes who play decent tennis. They left together. The start, I'm sure, of a beautiful friendship."

Evan was looking at her more closely now, his face a study in more emotions than Anne could count. His eyes sought hers as if questioning her response to his explanation. Billie Kanahele appeared with an ice bag and a glass of something cold and pink that she insisted be downed at once. Billie nodded her approval when Anne dutifully drank the sweet concoction. She took the glass from Anne, gave Evan a meaningful look, and said, "Mo' beddah not call da doctah, hey, Boss? She look okay now. Da kine. So maybe you let next door know she doin' okay, yeah? Da housekeeper dey got, she call two time already."

Anne frowned. "To ask about me?"

"How dey gonna know you here, you don't tell 'um?" Billie asked.

"Didn't you tell them Anne was here?" Evan asked.

The big woman shrugged impatiently, "How I'm supposed to know what you want, you didn't *told* me?"

Evan smiled indulgently as Billie clomped out of the bedroom, shaking her head as though her employer was a hopeless case. "I suppose they're worried about you next door. If you left in a huff, without telling anyone where you were going . . ."

Anne took the ice bag from her forehead. Her head was clear; she had stopped shaking. She swung her legs to the side of the bed, testing them gingerly on the floor. "I'd better let them know I'm all right," she said. She still felt a little unsteady as she got to her feet, but there was no need to remain in bed. "I'm sorry for all the trouble I've caused you," she told Evan. "I was . . . upset and . . . I guess the sun sort of . . . did me in."

"Sure you want to leave?" Evan asked. "I can call next door and tell them you're all right."

"That's all I'd need," Anne said. She forced a weak smile. "I run away from home and I come here."

"You didn't come here," he corrected. "I carried you. And it was hardly your idea."

"Still, if they're worried . . ."

"Do you care what they think?" Evan asked. He placed a hand on Anne's forearm.

Standing this close to Evan, she didn't care what anyone in the world thought. She wanted to be closer to him. She forced herself to avoid his eyes. "It's not right to have them thinking something may have happened to me. I'll go back."

"And expose yourself to a nice family scene? You could stay here, you know."

"Until the wedding?" Anne said cuttingly.

"Well, you're not going to stay at the Delons' and put up with what made you run out of the place."

"I'm still a guest," Anne said. "I can't blame Mrs. Delon for what Warren does. And I owe it to Larry to tell him what I'm going to do."

At the door, Evan closed his hands over Anne's shoulders and turned her around to face him. "What *are* you going to do, Anne?"

She lowered her head. "I don't know," she whispered. "Larry's done nothing to . . . nothing that should have changed my feelings about him. I just . . . I don't know what I'm going to do."

"You were going to let me know," Evan said. "I've been waiting."

Anne couldn't resist a cutting reminder. "You haven't been too lonely while you waited."

He looked puzzled for a moment and then Evan scowled. "Are you going to keep reminding me that I don't much care to sail alone? And that it's handy, when you're playing tennis, to have someone on the other side of the net? I told you I want you, Anne. But I also want to . . ." He stopped shortly.

"You want to what?"

"I want to respect you, too. I can't stand to see you letting those people walk all over you, rearranging your life while you stand by like that . . . that flabby-charactered female Warren's married to. If you can call that a marriage."

She felt too weak to protest. Even reminding Evan that she had run from the house today wouldn't have meant anything. She was going back. When she left, it wouldn't be like some hysterical schoolgirl, racing off without even knowing where she was going. Larry didn't deserve that. And Larry didn't deserve her standing here in Evan's bedroom with his hands on her shoulders, radiating a magnetism that would pull her against him in another instant. "I . . . I really must go," Anne whispered. "Thank you, again. And thank Billie for me, too."

"Is that all I get for rescuing a damsel in distress?" he smiled, letting one hand slide up to trace the delicate line of her cheek. "A polite little thank you?" He cupped her face in his hands and in that instant she swayed toward him, all thoughts of Larry pushed from her mind. He took her mouth gently in a series of drugging little kisses, leaving her aching for a more complete possession.

"Anne . . . Anne," he groaned against her

soft lips. "Why do you do it? This is torture for both of us. Stay here with me. . . . Let me love you." He crushed her to him as though he couldn't bear to let her go, his kiss a primitive force that could not be denied. She gave a little gasp at the fierceness of his passion, thrilling to the feel of his strong, hard body against hers. His hands spread waves of fire up and down her back, then moved around to cup her breasts, their warmth all too palpable through the thin cotton of her T-shirt. She moaned softly as his thumbs rubbed teasingly over her hardened nipples, stroking her body to a new state of arousal.

The emotion-laden events of the day were suddenly too much for her; this breathtaking assault on her senses more strain than her overwrought nerves could stand. Once again, she felt faint and dizzy, her entire body quivering in Evan's strong arms. Recognizing her weakness at once, Evan held her still against him, his embrace now more comforting than stimulating.

"Please . . ." she managed to whipser. "I've got to go . . ."

"I know, I'm sorry." His voice was oddly tender. "I should have realized you weren't yourself yet. Here," he motioned her toward the bed, "you'd better lie down again for a minute."

"No. No, I'm fine now, really." She knew that if she once lay down on his bed, she'd never have the strength to leave.

"All right," he said, placing a comforting arm round her shoulders, "I'll take you home, then. But I'll be in touch."

He walked her downstairs and then most of the way up the driveway to the gateposts. When they parted, he repeated, "I'll be in touch, Anne. If you need me, please call. I doubt Warren will do anything but sleep for a day or two. And he'll be on his good behavior now that his mother's been alerted. But if you feel uncomfortable, or . . . if you just want to talk to someone, I'll be here at home. And still waiting."

It was strange, the way she wanted to get away from Evan and yet felt lost and empty the minute he had turned to retrace his footsteps. She had wanted to get away because his power over her was too overwhelming. And, as she walked toward the Delon house, she had several moments when she wanted to run back to Evan, to have him clasp her again in his arms, to assure her that everything was going to be all right.

Amalia was on the driveway as Anne approached the house. She waved excitedly and ran inside. Apparently she had gone to tell Mrs. Delon that Anne was back, for Larry's mother came out to greet Anne, looking genuinely relieved. "Oh, my dear, you don't know how worried I was about you."

Anne apologized. "I just . . . wanted to get away and . . . calm myself down."

"I can quite understand." Mrs. Delon made

195

no maternal move toward her. She didn't link her arm with Anne's or put a friendly arm around her shoulders. But she escorted Anne into the living room and said, "I do wish you'd sit down a moment. I'll have Amalia bring some iced tea. Unless you'd rather have a drink?"

Mrs. Delon was in charge again. When Anne told her that she had no desire for a drink and wanted to go upstairs and lie down, the latter statement was ignored and Mrs. Delon summoned the maid to give her an order for two iced teas. She gestured at one of the long floral-print sofas, inviting Anne to sit down. "We *are* overdue for a little chat, and I must apologize. I've been so fearfully busy, we haven't really had a chance to get acquainted." She sat down beside Anne. "Or to iron out our little differences."

Anne said nothing, waiting for an explanation of their "little differences." She was annoyed with herself for having agreed to listen. Another of Millicent Delon's command performances, she thought grimly. Why hadn't she gone to her room?

"First, of course, I cannot tell you how sorry I am about Warren. When people drink, and, unfortunately, Warren does not drink very gracefully, they . . . well, I don't have to tell you that they are not themselves." Mrs. Delon made a dismissing gesture with her heavily beringed hand. "Lawrence would be devastated, as you know. I'm sure you will have the graciousness to forget whatever it was that happened this morning."

Anne sat still, tight-lipped.

"It would be a shame to throw a pall over the wonderful day we have planned. And poor Veronica has enough problems. Her health is none too good, you know." Mrs. Delon acted as though that settled the matter. She favored Anne with a wan smile and went on. "Now, as to some of your statements, which I know were made in the heat of anger and should be excused, but . . . I prefer to explore them. You made a reference to your background, as compared to that of my family. I do hope that you will not let an unfortunate little brush with . . . momentary irresponsibility . . . color your opinion of the family with whom you are going to share a . . . quite distinguished name."

"I wasn't putting down the family name," Anne said tersely. "I just wanted it known that I won't have Warren coming anywhere near me. Ever again."

For a few seconds, Mrs. Delon looked abashed. But she regained her superior attitude and said, "I think that can be assumed. And if I insist upon it, I am sure you will have Warren's apology. However, I do want it known that I have had to make some concessions, too."

"In accepting me?" Anne flared. "I don't want any favors, Mrs. Delon."

"I was not patronizing you, my dear. We are,

I believe, quite open-minded about people from outside our own social bracket. My son certainly proved that. And, while I will admit that I . . . I did have other plans for Lawrence, I am hardly a dictatorial woman. And Lawrence is quite his own man. Heaven knows I have plunged into plans for your wedding with all the enthusiasm possible."

"No one would deny that," Anne told her. "You've taken them over completely."

"There. You're finally coming out with it," Mrs. Delon said in a tone of triumph. "But you can scarcely say that I pushed you aside. I have never seen less interest on the part of a bride-to-be. You might blame that on the fact that we will be entertaining friends of Lawrence's family instead of your own. However, it is not our fault that you don't have a wide social circle of your own."

Something inside Anne wanted to scream. It was all true. Yes, everything Mrs. Delon was saying was true. And she was being honest now; she had even admitted that she had cherished other hopes for her younger son. Inez's name hovered between them, unspoken, Why don't I feel resentment when she tells me she would have preferred Inez Carruthers as her daughter-in-law? Anne wondered. Why don't I tell her what I think of what she has done to Veronica? Why don't I yell or cry or run out of the room instead of sitting here and listening to this detestable, artificial woman?

Anne knew why she didn't respond. Because Larry had become a virtual stranger to her. Because she had just left the company of a man whose mere touch set her senses on fire.

Amalia came into the room carrying a tray. She served the iced tea, gave Anne a quick questioning look, and was dismissed with a wave of Mrs. Delon's hand.

"I had really hoped," Mrs. Delon said after a cautious sip from her glass, "that you would . . . shall we say, enter into the spirit of this family. Frankly, I've been disappointed in your lack of interest."

"In your shopping trips, Mrs. Delon? In your luncheons with friends I don't even know?"

Mrs. Delon's eyes flashed at the thick sarcasm Anne had not even tried to disguise. "Well, I would have hoped that you would take some interest in the people who are Lawrence's friends and, equally important, his clients. But I was speaking of the . . . the social graces. Lawrence does like to play tennis, you know. He loves to sail. And you were provided with a . . . most cooperative teacher."

Something in Mrs. Delon's face, something in her eyes, something even more apparent in the precise way in which she said "most cooperative teacher" caught Anne's attention. Had she been promoting Anne's association with Evan Forrester deliberately? Had she seen the same things Veronica had seen, the way Anne lighted up when Evan came into a room? If she hadn't, Veronica or Inez, who lighted up the same way, had certainly pointed that fact out to Mrs. Delon. Had she been hoping to forestall a marriage she didn't approve of by pushing Anne toward Evan Forrester? Had she hoped to provide Larry with a reason for calling off the marriage?

Perhaps so, Anne thought. But certainly not at this late date. The invitations had been mailed by now. Mrs. Delon would not risk a scandal that would tarnish the family name and embarrass her before her friends. *Or would she?* She was clever. She was devious. And no one could doubt her lack of enthusiasm for the mere office worker who had won the heart of her handsome, successful, personable younger son. Warren Delon had not been much of a catch for any woman and his wife had bent easily to Mrs. Delon's direction. But Lawrence was another matter. And Anne had already told Mrs. Delon what she thought of the family.

Anne became aware that she had not responded to Mrs. Delon's remark about her sailing teacher. The older woman was staring at her with those pale blue eyes that, in spite of their washed-out color, managed to look piercing when she chose to question someone who didn't agree with her.

"Anne? I do wish you'd offer something in the way of a comment," Mrs. Delon said after a long silence. "I'd like not to believe the

. . . insinuations that have been made about you. I'd like to believe that Lawrence isn't going to be very deeply hurt."

Anne got to her feet, leaving her ice-tea glass on the table before her, untouched. "I don't know what sort of insinuations you've heard, Mrs. Delon. Or who made them. And I don't want to see Larry hurt anymore than you do."

She had started trembling again. Anne had hoped that her response would sound firm and strong, but conscience watered down her self-assurance. Mrs. Delon's questioning stare was unbearable.

"I'll be talking with Larry shortly," Anne finished. "If you like, I'll assure him that all the innuendos you've heard are just gossip. Stories from people who don't seem to have anything better to do."

There! She had sounded almost convincing. But, as Anne excused herself, truthfully telling Mrs. Delon that she felt faint and wanted to rest, Anne wished that she could have been totally honest. It would have been wonderful to deny that she was even remotely interested in any man but Larry. It would have been soul-satisfying to tell Mrs. Delon in no uncertain terms that she missed Larry with all her heart and was counting the days until they were husband and wife. But lies had not been a part of Anne's previous experience. She despised herself now for not being able to shout out a vigorous denial of the "insinuations." Most of all, she despised herself for not knowing where the real truth about her emotions lay.

"We must talk again," Mrs. Delon said.

Their conversation, like Anne's heart, was left dangling.

Chapter Twelve

T alking with Larry didn't solve Anne's dilemma, but his calm, self-possessed way of speaking had a way of bringing Anne back to reality. Their plans to marry were real, the wedding was only a few weeks off, he talked about their honeymoon and sounded sincere and sentimental in his repeated declarations of love.

Anne didn't mention the incident with Warren, nor Mrs. Delon's reference to "insinuations." Evan's name was not mentioned either. It was an unemotional, pleasant conversation that made Anne ashamed of her association with Evan Forrester. Larry's talk was of a shared future. What had Evan promised her? He was known as a womanizer. It seemed shoddy to have her thoughts so possessed by a man who probably prided himself on his ability to catch a woman's interest, making other men look dull and stodgy by comparison.

Yet, the next morning, when Warren *did* offer a grudging, mumbled apology, and when it seemed that Mrs. Delon and Inez were not

on the best of terms, following Inez's prolonged and unexplained absence from the
house, and just as Anne was starting an animated discussion with Mrs. Delon about the
floral decorations for the wedding, her heart
began to pound erratically as Evan Forrester
came strolling across the lawn from the back
of the garden.

A brisk wind ruffled his dark hair. He wore
white dungarees and a white nylon jacket
with the insignia of a local yacht club. And as
he neared the lanai, his deeply tanned face
creased with one of his devastating smiles.
"Good morning, neighbors."

Anne pretended a casualness she did not
feel. "Oh, hi, Evan."

His charm was not lost on Mrs. Delon.
"Good morning, darling. I see you're still leaping walls." She beamed at Evan. "Haven't you
learned your lesson? I've heard you nearly
flattened one of my lovely house guests doing
that."

"Yes, I did run into one of them," Evan said
evenly. "I came to see if she wants to take the
postgraduate course in sailing." He turned
his level gaze toward Anne. "You're fine in
good weather, but I can't call myself a good
teacher until you learn how to come about in a
frisky wind."

Anne saw a subtle, brow-lifting expression
on Mrs. Delon's face. Noncommittally, she
said, "We do seem to have a good bit of wind.
Unusual for this time of year." More point-
edly, she added, "I hope it blows itself out

before the wedding. Can you imagine a huge tent in the garden if the weather acts up?"

Anne pretended deep interest in a color brochure of floral arrangements from an orchid grower on the big island of Hawaii.

"Do I hear any takers?" Evan persisted.

"Thank you," Anne said with a primness that sounded ridiculous to her own ears. "But I . . . we're expecting Larry any day now. He said yesterday that he had just a few bits of business to finish up and he'd be on his way."

Evan shrugged. "I suppose I'll have to look around for someone else to handle the jib."

Amazingly, Mrs. Delon said, "Oh, nonsense. Lawrence and I talked just an hour ago and I know he's tied up for at least another day or two. He certainly isn't going to be here today. And what with my appointment at the hairdresser, and Veronica moping in her room, and Inez in one of her moods, Anne can't look forward to any stimulating company around here today." She looked brightly toward Anne, "It might be your last chance to learn the ropes, my dear. That's putting it quite literally, isn't it?" She released a tinny, unconvincing little laugh. "You'll want to impress Lawrence with your expertise when he arrives."

"I don't know . . ." Anne's confusion was like an ache in her chest. "I really . . . it might be interesting, but . . ."

"Oh, run along," Mrs. Delon insisted. Then, as if she didn't want it to appear as if she were encouraging more reasons for the insinuations she had heard, she said lightly, "I'm sure Evan's intentions are perfectly respectable. A man who takes his own housekeeper sailing can't have anything on his mind but seamanship."

"I'll have to think about that remark," Evan said. His dark eyes flashed a look of contempt, unseen by Mrs. Delon. "Meanwhile, my offer stands. And the sailing lessons, after all, were your idea, Millicent."

"Of course they were." Mrs. Delon took the florist's catalog from Anne. "I think we're in agreement on the archways, aren't we, Anne? Oh, they're going to be fantastic. Bowers and bowers of enormous white orchids!"

"I'm sure everyone will be impressed," Evan said. His eyes looked searchingly into Anne's. "Especially the bride."

Anne felt a rush of warmth. She hoped Mrs. Delon wouldn't notice her discomfiture. And then, to her own amazement, she was saying, "I think it would be fun. You're right, Evan. I've only handled the boat in calm weather."

"It might even be exciting," Evan said. His stare was challenging now.

Maybe it was only Anne's imagination, but it seemed to her that the atmosphere was charged with unspoken thoughts, unrevealed intentions.

"I'll have to change," Anne said, finally turning away from Evan's steady gaze. "I won't be long."

She left Evan and Mrs. Delon chatting about the strange turn in the weather. Hurrying up the stairs, she felt on the brink of some momentous adventure, a feeling that hovered between anticipation and dread.

As was usual when she was with Evan, Anne forgot completely about the strained atmosphere she had left behind her as soon as they reached the boat. The air was clear and cool, the ocean an untypically dramatic and choppy gray, the sun diffused by billowing clouds that hung low over the sea, hinting of rain. There was an electric tension in the air that went far beyond the unseasonal storm-threatening weather.

Out of the harbor, the sail flapping wildly, Evan's little sloop behaved like a wild bucking bronco. Her face and hair wet with salt spray, Anne was kept too busy to worry about what Mrs. Delon might think or not think about this unexpected excursion. But she was not too busy following Evan's sure orders to be unaware of his nearness. Now wearing only cutoff jeans, Evan seemed to be unaware of the devastating effect his lean, tanned, muscular body had on Anne. But every brush against him, every contact with his hands as he instructed Anne in the art of sailing through the choppy waters, was like an infusion of molten lava in her veins. She was breathless not only from the exertion of sailing the small sloop as she tacked her way along the coastline, but from the heady feeling of being close to Evan.

They were both dripping from the cool salt

spray, both working hard and breathing heavily, when a sudden lurch of the sloop threw Anne against Evan's chest. She started to move away, laughing self-consciously as a high swell threw her off balance. Evan made a choking sound, an impassioned groaning of her name, "Anne! Anne, my God, let's stop being children. I need you. I need you . . . and I want you!"

Steely arms pulled Anne close. Their sea-wet bodies pressed against each other. And Anne felt a sudden dizziness at the hard pressure against her hip. His masculinity was an obvious force, compelling and uncontrollable. Anne felt the blood hammering in her temples, her entire being was consumed by the fire of a demanding kiss that possessed her mouth.

They clung to each other for a long time in a desperate grip. This was not close enough, Anne knew. They would never be close enough.

How long did they remain locked in that passionate fusion? It could have been seconds and it could have been an eternity before Evan's husky, emotion-racked voice whispered in her ear, "Let's go someplace where we'll be more comfortable, darling."

Anne was too numbed by her racing desire to reply.

"Anne? Dearest—look at me!"

"I . . . can't." Seeing her own searing need reflected in Evan's eyes would have been too overwhelming. "I can't, Evan. I'm . . ."

"Look at me!" he commanded.

She forced herself to look up at the eyes that burned into her own like black coals. "Please! I'm so . . ."

"Confused? Are you going to tell me you're still confused?" Evan's words were harsh and angry, accompanied by a brutal tightening of his arms. "Damn it, you love me! Stop denying it! Stop lying to yourself! *You love me, Anne!*"

She could not bring herself to admit it to him, still fearful that this unbelievably handsome, excitingly virile man was only toying with her emotions.

He was suddenly tender, caressing her arms and back with his strong hands. "You've never been made love to before. Are you frightened, darling? I'll be gentle. I'll make love to you as though you were a fragile flower, a beautiful bud that hasn't opened yet. Do you hear what I'm saying? I have a crying need for your body, Anne, but I want more than that. I want you to love me. I don't want you to be afraid."

She was close to tears, feeling herself being swept away by a relentless tide, her fear less insistent than the crying need that had possessed her. Before Evan's penetrating gaze became too potent to be met, before she turned away from the dark eyes that were like searchlights into her very soul, Anne answered Evan's question, but she did it silently to herself. She *did* love this man. If this terrible, unquenchable need to be one with him was love, then she loved this man as she had never dreamed she was capable of loving. Larry Delon had become a cartoon figure without substance. He had never made her pulse throb with the hunger or the excitement that tore at her now and robbed of all will-power.

"We could go below," Evan was murmuring, his lips wet and salty against Anne's face. "Or we could go to the yacht. Let's do that, Anne. I've waited so long—I've got to have you And you want me. I know you want me."

They were making their way back to the harbor, skirting the barren, unpopulated southern end of the island, when the storm came upon them with a sudden fury. In the short time that they had been locked in that wild intimacy, the sky had turned a sullen gray, the wind had risen, and the waters around them had become a violent cauldron of water buffeting the tiny craft without mercy.

Evan let her go. He was like an alert animal, head held high as if to sense the danger they had abruptly encountered, his eyes bright with concern. "I don't like this," he said. "Anne . . . we're going to take down the sheets. This is crazy, but it's happening. We're going to have to ride it out."

The tremor of fear that ran through her was abated by Anne's confidence in Evan. "Just . . . tell me what to do."

He gave orders. Anne followed them, holding on to her precarious footing on the small deck as a strong wind blew up and tipped the sloop so that the starboard rail was slicing through the sea. The sound of the canvas, as Anne helped Evan strip the mast, was like furious gunfire.

"Beautiful," Evan encouraged. He was at the tiller, trying to bring them to rights when the furious gust of wind startled them both, sending a pang of terror through Anne. It was followed by a loud cracking sound and Evan's warning cry, "Look out!" He made a mad lunge toward her, his arms pulling Anne toward the stern as the mast splintered and toppled across the deck. It had missed her by inches. Anne shivered as Evan pressed her close to the safety of his broad chest.

Holding Anne close, nuzzling his face against her cheek, Evan said, "That was too close. Too close." He surveyed the broken mast. It lay across the deck for a few seconds. Then an insane tipping motion sent it sliding into the sea, leaving behind it a splintered stub where the mast and sail had been. "Oh, great!" Evan said, following his words with a barely audible curse. The wind was screaming, a shrill whine over the slamming sound of water against the fragile hull. "You're not afraid, are you, dear? There's nothing to be afraid of."

"I'm not afraid," Anne told him. It was only half true. The darkness that had come over them, the strident pitch of the wind, the helplessness of the tiny vessel as it was swept over by one furious sea after another, were terrifying. Yet, with Evan's arms around her, with his bold, assured voice saying, "We'll ride it out. It's going to be all right," Anne was less afraid. She leaned against the strength of him, breathing a prayer.

Huddled together in the well as the wild waves washed over the now incapacitated sloop, they began the process of "riding it out." The terror seemed to be without an end. Bobbing up and down on the churning water, the thin wail of the wind assaulting their ears, they remained powerless for uncounted hours, their balance threatened by the rigging that attached the broken mast to the side of the ship until Evan, braving gusts that threatened to sweep him overboard, cut them free of the broken mast and the now useless sail.

It could have been midnight, except that there were no stars above them, only a depressing blackness that had once been the beautiful blue Hawaiian sky. Holding Anne close to him, pressing her reassuringly against his body as each chilling swell washed over the sloop, Evan kept up his words of encouragement. "Don't worry, Anne. We'll make it back. Just . . . let me hold you close and be patient."

It was half dream and half nightmare. The nightmare was a terrifying wind and a constant assault of water washing over them as the sloop danced insanely over the turbulent sea. The dream? The dream was the power of Evan's confidence, the strength of his body holding Anne in a tight embrace that made her feel as though she were a part of him. He was not afraid. How could she feel any fear while he held her in his arms?

There was no way of knowing whether it was night or day when the sloop, barely missing an outcropping of lava rocks, washed close to an isolated beach, finally turning over on its side like a dying animal some twenty yards from the sand. His arm around Anne's waist, Evan guided her through the swirling waters, their heads down against the wind, as they struggled toward the shore. With the enveloping darkness came a burst of torrential rain. Anne looked back over her shoulder to see the dim outlines of Evan's little sloop being buffeted against an outcropping of rocks. Over the roar of the rain and the wind, she moaned, "Oh, Evan . . . your little boat!"

"It's replaceable," Evan shouted. "You're not." As they waded through the frothing surf, then touched the wet sand, Evan added bitterly, "I must have been out of my mind, exposing you to this. Selfish. I just wanted to be with you."

They were on the thinly inhabited end of the island, where the road was barely traversable, where the beaches were rough and almost always deserted. Through the deluge, Evan guided Anne to a brush covered hill. Climbing upward, Anne asked, "Where are we going?"

"Up, where the incoming tide won't get us," he said. "There used to be a little shack up here. Are you all right?"

Anne nodded. "Don't worry about me."

Evan gave her waist a warm squeeze. "That's my girl."

Through the heavy rain, they made out the shadowy outlines of a small frame building. It jutted out from the hilltop without the grace of trees or shrubs to blend it into the landscape. "Used to be a rangers' cabin," Evan said, his breath coming hard from the exertion. "At least we'll be dry."

The door was unlocked; Evan kicked it open with his knee and they entered a dank, musty room furnished with two rickety looking cots, a table and two splintered chairs. There was a stripped area that must, at one time, have served as a kitchen. Bare wooden floors and walls looked dusty and weatherworn; the dark ceiling was festooned with cobwebs.

"It's not the Ritz," Evan said, "but the roof doesn't seem to leak." He kicked the door shut. What little light there was from the cabin's single window hardly illuminated the room.

Anne shivered. She was wet and cold, but grateful to be alive, grateful to be out of the storm. Overhead, the rain beat down with a driving force.

Evan stripped one of the green cotton spreads from a cot, using it to wrap Anne's body and to pat her dry. "I can't tell you how sorry I am," he said. His touch, as he pressed the fabric against Anne's body, was gentle and impersonal. When Evan was satisfied that she was no longer dripping with cold water, he said, "Get out of that bikini. You can use this other bedspread as a wrap."

"What about you?" Anne asked. He was still wearing the soaking, cutoff jeans.

"I'll dry off." He laughed shortly. "I'll turn around while you get out of your suit." He walked over to the window to watch the rain.

Anne slipped out of the bikini panties and then removed the top, still shivering. Then, unglamorously wrapped in the faded old cotton spread, she said, "Okay. I'm decent."

She turned to see that Evan had gotten rid of his wet trunks, catching her breath at the sight of his nakedness.

Evan let her stare at him for a few seconds and then said, "I don't want to shock you."

Anne felt her face burning. "You . . . wrap yourself in one of the blankets."

"Why?" He crossed the room and closed his arms around Anne. "Why? Are we still going to be coy? On my yacht, in a hotel room—wherever, darling—we would have ended up this way. I wish the setting were more glamorous for you, Anne, but . . . for my part, I'm just happy to be here with you. Just the two of us, alone—the way we've both wanted it."

Anne was quivering now, not from the chill, but from the remembered sight of Evan's maleness, the closeness of his powerful body as the thin cloth that separated them slipped away and brought flesh against flesh. She heard herself moan as Evan's lips found hers, searching, probing, possessing with an ardent hunger that brought a heated response. It was all strange and bewildering: the cabin, the darkness, the thunderous sound of rain pelting the roof. Evan's hands were exploring her body, his mouth showering kisses over her face, her neck, then her throat. He had stooped down to nuzzle her breasts with his lips. Anne felt herself slipping out of the mundane world, transported on a wave of undeniable passion. He was right. She wanted him as much as he seemed to want her.

"This is all that matters," he whispered huskily as his lips returned to her face. "Forget what's happened, forget where we are. This is all that matters, darling."

Anne was lifted off the floor in a swoop of powerful, naked arms. She kept her eyes pressed shut as Evan carried her to one of the cots, putting her down gently, and then covering her naked body with his own. "Anne . . . oh, Anne, if you only knew how I've dreamed about this . . . of how we belong together, a part of each other!"

She felt his nakedness pressing down against her bared body, his desire for her strong and hard against her thighs. "Evan . . . please! I don't . . . I don't think we . . ."

It was a feeble protest that was brushed aside by the raging heat of Evan's kisses raining on her body, his breathing coming in short, ecstatic gasps that had the ring of anguish. "Anne . . . Anne . . . Anne . . ." He repeated her name, his lips murmuring against her body. "Love me, darling! Love me . . . the way I love you . . ." He locked her more closely to him, kissing her lips, holding her down until she fell into a swooning helplessness. "*Want* me, Anne! Want me the way I want you! Tell me . . . tell me that you do!"

She was aware, now, only of a need to be held closer, to be possessed, to be a part of this incredible man whose desires she could no longer deny, who had awakened in her a searing need to be fused with him as though they were one. She was gasping for breath, feeling the slow, sensuous writhing of her body warm against his, knowing, somehow, that this was the moment for which she had been created. "I . . . Evan . . . I do," Anne whispered. Whatever might come later no longer mattered. There was only this rapturous moment in time. "I do want you . . . but I . . ."

"Anne—dearest—trust me," Evan said in a throaty half whisper.

Evan took his time. His kisses burned against Anne's mouth. His hard-muscled body was at once insistent and controlled, holding back until she was on the verge of screaming with her desire for him. No other lover could have inflamed her senses to this fever pitch. She was torn between crying out her frustration and taking the initiative, seizing him and drawing him close and making him an integral part of her.

Then, as suddenly as he had swept her to

the cot, Evan's body tensed. He lifted his face from Anne's, alert, as though listening for something.

Anne heard it, too. Over the now hushed sound of the rain, she caught the sound of a motor. The roar came closer and closer, until she felt that the noise would envelop the cabin. She stiffened, feeling Evan move away from her. Then she heard him say, "That's a helicopter."

Anne nodded, recognizing now the ear-splitting sound.

Evan had moved to sit on the side of the cot. "I can't imagine a pilot taking a chopper up in this weather." He made a suddering motion. Anne noticed that his body was gleaming with perspiration, shining like polished copper.

Anne averted her gaze as Evan got up from the cot. She heard him padding across the floor, then pulling open the door. She blinked her eyes at the sudden light. It was still dimly gray outdoors, but even that light contrasted with the darkness of the cabin's interior.

"Coast Guard," she heard Evan say. "I hope they see me." He was quiet, then. Apparently he had gone outside. A short while later, the door closed and Anne heard Evan say, "I don't think I got outside in time."

The helicopter had apparently circled the cabin area once or twice and then had gone on. There was only the sound of rain now.

"Were they looking for us, do you think?" Anne had sat up in the cot, the green bedspread pulled up to her shoulders. She still couldn't bring herself to look at Evan. His wet cutoff jeans were draped over the back of one of the chairs.

"I'm sure no chopper pilot in his right mind would be out joy-riding in this weather," Evan said. "Yes. Yes, I'm sure they're looking for us."

Anne felt him drop to the edge of the cot. "They must have seen the sloop. The wreckage."

"Nothing we can do about that now. I should have gotten outside faster and hailed them." Evan's hands caressed Anne's bare shoulders. "But while we're here . . ."

Anne felt rigid. The torrid sensations that had been burning inside her a few moments ago had chilled with the realization that the Delon family had alerted the Coast Guard. They were probably worried sick, and it would be worse when the helicopter pilot reported that Evan's sloop had capsized. *Larry.* By now, his mother had probably alerted Larry. She had to let them know that she was safe.

"Anne?" Evan's hands had stopped their massaging motion. His face was directly over Anne's, his eyes questioning. "Why the sudden chill?"

Anne pressed her eyes shut for a second and shook her head back and forth. "I'm sorry. I . . . can't help thinking about . . . people being worried about us."

"There's nothing we can do about that."

"The rain seems to be letting up," Anne said, listening closely.

"Not enough," Evan said.

"But we could get to a road, couldn't we?" Anne pressed the coverlet close to her skin. "There's got to be a house near by. Someplace where we can get to a phone."

"Not on this end of the island," Evan told her. "And there's no way to get to the road. Not now."

"But that's ridiculous! There's got to be a way. The rangers, or whoever used to use this cabin, had to have some kind of access."

"In dry weather, yes. But between this hill-top and the road, there's a gulley . . . in fact, there are two, that become torrents following a rain. Water washes down from the mountains. In a matter of minutes, you have white water . . . looks like the Colorado River at its wildest."

"I can't believe . . ."

"Then don't believe me!" Evan exploded. He got to his feet. Anne heard him stamping across the room. When he spoke again, she looked up to see him standing near her, wrapped in a flimsy blanket from the other bed. "Preserving modesty," he said. He tried laughing, but the laughter died quickly. Anne saw his dark eyes light with annoyance. "You can't leave here until hours after the rain stops, Anne. I thought we could make the best of a bad situation. I was thinking . . . maybe it happened for a reason. It was very beautiful."

Anne felt near tears. "It's just that . . ."

"Your mind is somewhere else?" Evan crossed the room to stare out the window at the grayness outside. "You can't let yourself go, can you? You've got to tease and torment and . . . all the while, you're still locked into that stupid situation you got yourself into. I want to make love to you and you're still thinking about what somebody else may be thinking!"

"Are you going to crucify me because I'm considerate? Because I don't want people to think I've been drowned?"

"Were you worried about that when we came in here? You were ready. You were more than willing to give yourself to me! Weren't your precious Delons worried about you *then*?"

His lack of understanding was unbelievable. Incensed, Anne cried out, "You always throw that at me, don't you? I'm human and I respond, and then you make me sound like . . . like some cheap little . . ."

"Like a woman!" Evan yelled. "Like a normal woman who's in love with a man!"

She had to strike back somehow. "You're always so sure of yourself!" She sounded more bitter than she felt.

"Tell me I'm wrong, then!" Evan shouted, whirling around to face her. His face was livid with rage. "Damn you, I've had it with your indecisiveness, your neurotic moods!"

"Oh, now I'm neurotic!" Anne wanted to leap out of the cot, but her nakedness kept her motionless. "I just happen to care about other people and how they feel. If you had any consideration . . ."

"I don't have that," Evan growled. "Go on! What other nice, fair observations do you want to make about me?"

"People think we're dead and all you can think about is . . . is . . ."

"Satisfying my animal lust?" Evan's voice filled the cabin with fury. "Is that what you're thinking?" He came back to the bed, this time grabbing Anne's shoulders with a painful grasp. "What kind of honeymoon were you expecting, with a man you obviously don't love? Was it all going to be proper and civilized, like a board of directors' meeting at Delon and Withrow? You were willing to go to bed for the rest of your life with a man you don't really know. A man you don't love! Don't love! Don't . . ."

"Stop it!" Anne shrilled. "I heard you the first time!"

"And it's true, isn't it? That's why you're getting hysterical—because you know it's true! If you had ever been in love with Larry Delon, you wouldn't have given me the time of day! What's more, if you had been welcome in that family, Millicent Delon wouldn't have pushed you at me, *hoping* you'd fall in love with me!"

Anne's breath congealed in her lungs. She was sick with humiliation. "That . . . that's not true!"

"Isn't it? You don't know how hard she's

pushed to get Larry and Inez married. She's not tough enough to buck Larry. After all, he's the one who keeps the family fortune rolling in. But if you talk to her long enough, you'll know that you're only being tolerated. And she'd give anything to get rid of you!"

"I'm not interested in what Mrs. Delon thinks!" Anne cried, "Larry's the only one . . ."

"Larry's the *what*?" Evan had started a sudden pacing of the small cabin. "The man you think about night and day? The one you were thinking about a little while ago when you told me you wanted me, the way I want you? You're a fool, Anne! You've made a terrible mistake and you don't even have the guts to admit it!"

Anne wrapped the old green bedspread around her nakedness and swung her legs to the floor. "I don't have to listen to this! I don't care what you do, I'm getting out of here!" She was marching over to where she had hung her bikini panties and bra when Evan grabbed her arms.

"You're not going anywhere! I just told you it's not safe!"

"I suppose taking me out into a storm was safe," Anne accused. It was an unfair, low strike at him. She realized that before the words were out of her mouth.

Evan's face was grim. He spun her around, almost flinging Anne back to the cot. "I'll try to forget that you said that. But you're still not going out there. It would be suicide to try to cross one of those runs. You're staying right where you are!"

She was seething with anger now, but Evan's attitude made it plain that it would do no good to argue. "For how long, Mr. Forrester?"

"Until I tell you it's safe to leave," he said. Anne dropped to the cot, wrapping herself in the bedspread, turning around to face the dingy wall as she heard Evan say, "I'm getting out of this ridiculous blanket. By all means keep your eyes averted. You might be disappointed because I'm no more interested in having you now than you are in having me!"

It had been gray and gloomy when they entered the cabin, but as Anne lay rigid on the cot, the light diminished. Could it really be nightfall? There was no letup in the deluge from the sky. Rain pelted the roof, creating a hushed sound in the tiny space, a sound that accelerated at times and imitated the fearsome rush of a freight train. There was no sound from Evan.

After a long while, frightened, Anne called out his name. From the opposite side of the room, she heard him respond with an unpleasant, "Yes?"

"I just . . . I just wanted to know that . . . you're still here."

"Of course I'm here. Go to sleep. I promise I won't bother you." He could not have sounded more cold.

Anne lay deathly still, listening to the storm, wishing she did not feel so completely lost and alone. Evan's nearness plagued her. How much more comforting it would be to have his arms holding her tight—to feel the warmth of his body and to hear reassuring words instead of the curt, hateful sounds that had just come from him!

But Anne thought of Larry, too. Larry being called and told that she had disappeared with Evan Forrester during a heavy storm—that their small boat had been spotted, turned over and without a mast, off an isolated beach. She felt ashamed of all the troubles she had already caused Larry. Surely he had been upset by reports that Anne seemed disinterested in their wedding reception, that she was not adjusting to the role of a Delon wife. It was unlikely that Larry had heard about the disturbing encounters with his brother, but even the incidents with Warren preyed on Anne's mind. And now this! If only there were some way to get to a telephone! But to go out in the rain and darkness, wrapped in a thin cotton covering, chancing the dangers Evan had warned her about? No, he was probably right. She would have to wait out the storm. But how long?

She knew that Evan was awake; every once in a while a throat-clearing sound or a deep sigh came to Anne from the opposite side of the room. He didn't trust her. He was sure she would attempt to do something foolish. And, as tired as he must be, he was staying awake to make certain that Anne didn't attempt to leave the cabin alone.

Annoyance with Evan subsided. Anne was finally aware only of his closeness. He would probably forget about her completely once they got out of this predicament. His disgust with her had been so strong that he had shaken physically while telling her what he thought of her. But Anne remembered more than his fury. She was haunted by the steely hardness of Evan's body, of the ecstasy he had invoked in her with the caress of his hands. And several times, before she drifted off into a troubled sleep, she came close to calling out his name and asking him to take the few steps across the room that would bring them together.

Chapter Thirteen

*A*nne awoke as the dawn filled the cabin with a dim, gloomy light. It took her several seconds to orient herself, to remember where she was and how she had come to be sleeping naked with only an unfamiliar green cotton cover to conceal her naked body.

Evan was awake, seated on the edge of the cot on the opposite side of the room, dressed in his cutoff jeans, looking toward Anne expectantly. Embarrassed, Anne responded to his, "Good morning!" without enthusiasm.

He seemed less angry now, saying, "The bad news is that there's probably a search out for us. The good news is that it hasn't been raining for hours."

Anne couldn't face him. "Does that mean we can go?"

"We can try," was all Evan promised. "I've been waiting for you to wake up."

Shortly afterward, still feeling nude in her damp bikini, Anne followed Evan down the hill and across a muddy expanse that had apparently been a raging river several hours earlier. They made their way to the highway, barely exchanging a word. Feeling messy, hungry, and depressed, Anne trudged beside Evan until they came to the first sign of civilization, a rustic house all but hidden by towering papaya trees and brilliant bougain-villaea vines. She waited outside while Evan knocked and was admitted into the house. She felt as though she wanted to hide when Evan came out a few moments later accom-panied by a long-haired blond surfer-type. The young man gave Anne a surprised look as Evan told her that he had arranged for them to be driven home.

There was almost no conversation during the drive to the Delon estate, except for the young man's occasional comments about the storm. "Wow! I heard on the radio it was the worst rain in sixty-six years. You guys are lucky you found a place to take shelter." He said nothing about an alarm for two missing persons thought to have been lost at sea.

In the Delon's driveway, Evan said, "Do you want me to come inside with you? Help you explain?"

"I think it's going to be bad enough going in alone," Anne told him. She had never before felt more miserable. Her bare feet were caked with mud; she knew she looked bedraggled and hopelessly disheveled.

Evan said, "I'm sorry, Anne. I meant it to be a wonderful day."

Anne's eyes flooded with tears and she nodded. Still unable to look directly at Evan, she let him help her out of the battered old surf wagon. She heard the car sputter out of the driveway, bound for the house next door, as she walked to the side entrance.

She walked into bedlam. Mrs. Delon, seeing her, shrieked, "Oh, I can't believe it! I simply can't believe it!"

Feeling exposed and too ill at ease to look anyone in the eye, Anne started a halting description of what had happened.

"We've been frantic," Mrs. Delon interrupted. She was joined in the lanai by Veronica and Warren, then by a cold-faced Inez. They were all staring at her as though Anne was a bug under a microscope. She wished, fervently wished, that the ground would open up and swallow her.

"Couldn't you have telephoned?" Mrs. Delon was asking. Then she added the *coup de grace*. "Lawrence is here. He's been on the telephone all morning. How could you upset us this way? *How could you do this to us?*"

"I . . ." Anne made a shuddering motion. "I'd like to get cleaned up. Then I'll tell you what happened."

"Should be an interesting story," Warren sneered.

His mother glared at him. Veronica said something vaguely sympathetic, and Anne was starting toward the stairway when Larry hurried onto the lanai.

There was a terrible pause while he looked

her over, his face registering more disgust than concern. "Anne! Where have you been? Why didn't you let us know you were safe?"

Larry hadn't rushed over to take her in his arms or expressed his joy that she was still alive. He kept looking at her with an expression of distaste. Smart in a pale blue leisure suit, immaculately groomed as always, he made Anne feel like some loathesome thing that had washed up on the beach.

Anne opened her mouth to tell him that a telephone call had been impossible. She started to describe the harrowing escape from the storm. But Larry's eyes, critical and shocked at the sight of her, changed Anne's mind. She was beyond explanations, She no longer cared what any of these people thought about her. And worst of all was her guilt; whatever they were thinking, they were only technically wrong. She would have given herself to Evan last night except for the disturbance of a searching helicopter. "I . . . want to go upstairs," she said faintly.

Finally, there was some show of concern for her. It came from Veronica. "You must have had a terrible time of it. Come on, Anne. I'll go upstairs with you."

"Yes. Must have been quite a night," Warren said.

Larry shot him a baleful look, but he still didn't come near Anne.

And Mrs. Delon, looking stunning in one of her exotic printed dashikis, made a dramatic gesture with her ringed hands. "To put us through the agony we've gone through! Not to let us know you weren't dead! I've never been exposed to such lack of consideration! A simple call . . ."

"There wasn't anyplace from which to call!" Anne cried.

Mrs. Delon's eyes narrowed. "There is no place on this island where one cannot make contact," she accused.

"The rangers' cabin is one of them!" Anne protested hotly. "Until the rain stopped . . ."

"Until the rain stopped, it must have been quite cozy," Inez said. She gave Larry a snide look, smiling faintly, then turned and walked toward the living room.

"I can't believe it," Larry muttered. He looked pained. "I simply can't believe this of you, Anne."

Mrs. Delon was glaring at Anne openly now. "Just look at you! Aren't you ashamed to . . . ?"

"I'm not ashamed!" Anne heard herself shriek. "I went through a terrible ordeal. We barely escaped with our lives! And all any of you can do is . . . is stare at me and tell me you can't believe it! Well, I can't believe any of you either!"

"Anne, really," Larry said in an irritatingly placid tone. "Mother's been up all night worrying about you. I've just gotten off a plane. We're exhausted, and you might have the kindness not to . . ."

"Not to what? Tell you what I think of you?" All the accumulated snubs and frustrations mounted up inside Anne, like hot lava bubbling up inside a volcano and demanding an explosive release. "Not one of you has asked if I'm hurt . . . if I'm all right . . . if Evan's even alive! All you care about is yourselves—how it's going to look . . ."

"We know how it looks," Mrs. Delon snapped. "You had an all-night tryst with our neighbor, that's exactly how it looks. In a . . . you admitted it yourself . . . in some shoddy cabin, probably not more than a mile or two from where you could have telephoned us for a car!"

Anne returned the pale-eyed, malevolent stare. Then she looked to Larry, to see if he would come to her defense. All she got from him was an uneasy look that said he wished people didn't make scenes—he wished his fiancée didn't look like a mud-spattered tramp.

"It wasn't a . . . 'tryst,' Mrs. Delon. We did the best we could in an emergency. Evan can tell you better than I can why we couldn't get to a telephone."

"I'm sure he can," Warren commented, staring at the rim of his cocktail glass.

There was another exchange of hateful looks among the family members.

"You'd know," Anne hurled at Warren. "If there's a nasty interpretation to be made, you'd be the first to understand it." She turned back to Mrs. Delon. "And you'd back him up. Anything to save your precious family reputation."

"Anne, I don't think that . . ."

Larry's words only aggravated her. "You don't know what I'm talking about because it's been kept from you."

Mrs. Delon gasped. "Oh, Lawrence . . . Lawrence . . . how could you have inflicted this upon us?"

Larry looked down at the floor. "Mother, I'm sure Anne can explain . . ."

"I'm not explaining anything!" Anne cried. Her hand had gone to the engagement ring on her finger. Twisting it off, she thrust it out toward Larry. "And you won't have to apologize for me any longer. Here. It was a mistake, Larry. A terrible mistake from the word go. And now you're free to find someone in your own social and financial class. Someone who won't embarrass you or send your mother into hysterics."

The ring was dropped into Larry's hand. He accepted it reluctantly, it seemed, but he didn't argue. He seemed more concerned about his mother, who was suddenly pacing the lanai like a heroine in a melodrama, wringing her hands together and saying, "Oh, what did we do to deserve this? Invitations in the mail! Our friends coming from all over the world . . . and now *this!*"

"You should be enormously relieved," Anne told her. She lifted her head in the air, oblivious to how she looked, and marched past the others. "I'll be out of here as fast as I can. And Larry isn't the only one who made a mistake,

Mrs. Delon. I nearly made one that would have ruined my life!"

She was out of the lanai, hurrying to the stairway, barely hearing the consternation she had left behind her. They were engaged in a stunned family conference. Anne didn't want to hear it.

It took only minutes to shower and get into clean clothes. That done, Anne telephoned the local airport, made a reservation for a flight to Honolulu, and then booked a flight from Honolulu to Los Angeles. She didn't know where she was going. Home? She had no home. No job, no one to turn to, no one she wanted to be with. She felt embarrassed for herself and for Larry. She wished she had never met him. But there was no heartbreak or remorse about their broken relationship as she started tossing clothes into her luggage. She left most of the items Larry had bought for her hanging in the closet. She had no regrets; she wanted no obligations or reminders.

She was almost finished with her packing, and had less than two hours before her flight from Maui, when there was a knocking on her door. Veronica, she suspected. Veronica had understood. She might not have known exactly what had happened, but she had put herself into Anne's place and she had empathized.

It wasn't Veronica. Anne opened the door to see Larry standing out in the hall, looking gray and somewhat sheepish.

"Anne? May I speak to you for a moment?"

He looked weary and distraught and Anne felt a pang of pity for him. Strange. This man who had seemed so far above her, looked only pitiable now, a small cog in his mother's social machine, someone who lacked the strength and independence to speak out for what he wanted and believed in. Anne nodded. "Come in," she said listlessly.

Larry nodded at the suitcase on the bed. "You're leaving?"

"I shouldn't have come," Anne told him. "It's not your fault, Larry. I didn't fit in here. I didn't belong. You'll be much better off when I go."

"No!" Anne was startled by the vehemence of his protest. "No, Anne. I didn't make a mistake and neither did you. I loved you for . . . for your refreshing honesty. I shouldn't have doubted you for an instant. I was . . . tired and I'd been worried sick. And when I saw you . . ."

"When you saw me, I didn't look quite like a Delon bride," Anne taunted. "And you were perfectly willing to believe the worst about me."

"I was . . . in a state of shock," Larry said. He stood awkwardly near the bed. "All night long, not knowing if you were dead or alive . . ."

"But when you found I was alive, you had only contempt for me," Anne said.

"No! No, please believe me, dear, it wasn't

contempt. I was just . . . embarrassed by all the things the others were saying . . . implying. And they're wrong. I know they're wrong, Anne. Can't we . . . go back to where we were?"

"Because the invitations have been mailed? Because we don't want to disappoint your mother's friends?" Anne tossed a striped tank top into her suitcase. "I don't want to marry you, Larry. Not because of what happened this morning but . . ."

He was looking at her like a melancholy child. "Because you don't love me?"

Anne forced herself to meet his eyes. "Yes, Larry. Because I don't love you. And I'll tell you something else. You . . . you've admired my honesty. Well, I haven't been all that honest. Your family's implied that I spent the night in . . . some kind of wild orgy last night. That's not true."

"I know that!" Larry exclaimed. "Anne, whatever made you think I'd believe that about you?"

"Let me get to my point," Anne said. "Larry, last night I didn't . . . I didn't . . ." She lowered her eyes, embarrassed, but determined to tell Larry the truth. Anne took a deep breath, looked directly at Larry and said, "Evan didn't make love to me last night, but it's only because there was an interruption. A helicopter flew over the cabin. When Evan got back, I was out of the mood. I was worried about you, about how concerned you would be. What I'm trying to say is, I resisted him because I felt guilty, not because I didn't want him. I did. It's too late now, but I still do. And I think you ought to know, too, that your mother made it all very convenient. She must have been hoping I'd fall in love with Evan; anyone can tell you that she promoted the idea of our spending time together."

Larry looked as though the blood had been drained from him. He stared into space, looking past Anne as though she were not in the room.

"I'm not blaming her. It was one of those things," Anne went on. "And I'm truly sorry, Larry. You've been very good to me and I wished it had worked, but it's impossible. Maybe I'm so confused that I don't even know what real love is. But I wouldn't have been attracted to another man if I had really been in love with you. And, since you left me here with your family, I've realized I'm not right for you either." She didn't want to patronize him or placate him. Anne meant it as she said, "You deserve the best, Larry. Someone who really loves you. I'm not that woman."

Larry got up and went to the door, looking dazed. "You're sure, Anne? Are you absolutely sure? This could be an infatuation. The man's . . . extremely attractive. And I left you alone for too long . . ."

"I'm sure," Anne said. "I'm going back to the mainland. I'll find some sort of job and . . . try to start all over."

At the door, Larry paused. "What will your . . . friendly sailing instructor have to say about that?"

Anne ignored the bitterness in Larry's voice. "He hasn't ever made any promises, Larry. He's . . . just someone I shouldn't have met. The way you shouldn't have met me."

Evan would have become furious. He would have raved and ranted, throwing accusations at Anne, telling her how wrong her decision was, reminding her of how much they cared for each other. Larry only hesitated in the doorway for a moment and said, "When you're ready, Anne, I'll get you to the airport. You know, of course, that this is very painful for me. And it's going to be terribly embarrassing for Mother."

That was what was important to all of the Delons, Anne realized. They could be emotionally distraught, but their first thought would always be for appearances. She felt sorry for Mrs. Delon, but a wedding could be called off with less effort than it had been engineered. The burning irony was that Larry had just seen the end of a lifetime commitment and his only reaction had been a final comment that revealed his weakness, his shallowness. It was going to be "terribly embarrassing for Mother." Anne shook her head. "If you don't mind, Larry, I'd rather get to the airport alone. That way, we'll save ourselves the . . . awkwardness of having to say good-bye."

Larry stood and thought about that for a

moment. Then he nodded and said, "This is terrible. This is . . . unthinkable!" Then he had gone. The door was closed. Anne returned to her packing.

Not five minutes could have elapsed before there was another knock on her door. "Larry? I'm packing and I don't have much time left . . ." She didn't want to see him again. There was nothing left to say. And Anne realized that there never *had* been much to say, except polite banalities.

"It's not Larry." Veronica's voice was followed by a more insistent rapping on the door.

Anne hurried to open it. Veronica made no attempt to smile or to pretend that all was well. "I won't keep you long," she said. "But I did want to say good-bye. And to offer to drive you to Kahalui. Larry just told us that you don't want to go with him."

Still dutifully reporting every detail to his mother, Anne thought. "That's very kind of you, but . . . can you understand why I might want to go alone?" Veronica had followed her into the room. "Why I don't want any sticky farewell scenes?"

Veronica came over to the edge of the bed. "Yes. Yes, I think I can understand that. If I were leaving, if I had half your strength, Anne, I'd want to go that way, too. Just disappear." She smiled faintly, looking directly at Anne with a touchingly sad expression. "*If* I were leaving, that is." Her hazel eyes told Anne that she wished she could. "Well, you'll be spared a 'farewell scene,' as you call it, with Mrs. Delon. She's gone to her room with strict orders that she not be disturbed. She'll have a big day ahead of her tomorrow, canceling all those orders and contacting all the wedding guests."

"I feel terrible about that," Anne admitted. "But I . . ."

"You've done what you had to do," Veronica said. "I . . . wanted to explain what I said to you before—about being sorry you came here. You stirred things up, Anne. You did more than make me jealous. You made me see what a stupid little toady I've been all these years. People hate it when they're faced with having to make a change. And I have to. I don't know yet how, or when, but there's going to be a change."

"I didn't come to completely upset this family," Anne said.

"I've talked to my brother in Georgia. He can create a job in his company for Warren, if Warren wants it. I'm going to present him with that option tonight. Either we start living like a normal, sober, independent married couple, strictly on our own, or . . ." Veronica shrugged. "Pray that I'll have your strength, Anne. You don't even know where you're going, or do you? You'll have to . . . I suppose you'll have to find a job. I won't have to worry about things like that."

"Have you told Mrs. Delon about your plan?" Anne asked. She kept folding clothes and tucking them into the suitcase on the bed.

"No. For once, I'm going to do something

alone and then let her find out about it after-
wards." Veronica was quiet for a few seconds,
but she hovered near the bed as though she
had something more to say. Finally, she
asked, "Have you said good-bye to Evan?"

"I . . . don't think he wants any farewells
either," Anne said. "Please tell him that for
me, Veronica. I've been as unfair to him as
I've been to Larry . . . to Mrs. Delon. Because
I haven't known my own mind." Anne released a long sigh. "I've really made a mess of
things, for everybody."

"You could phone him," Veronica suggested.

"No. No. After what happened, after . . . he
let me know how disgusted he was with me, I
couldn't do that."

"He loves you," Veronica said bluntly.

Anne was startled, "How do you . . . what
makes you say that?"

"Because I know him. Surely he must have
told you that?"

"Yes, but . . . you told me this yourself. How
many other women have heard the same
thing from him?"

"None under this roof," Veronica said point-
edly. "And I doubt that there are any others.
You're a fool if you don't let him know you're
leaving, Anne. If I were you, if I thought he
cared one whit about me, I'd . . ." Veronica
didn't finish her sentence. "Oh, I'd better let
you go. Can I help you in any way? Pack some
of your things or . . . call a cab?"

"I've got the packing pretty well under control," Anne said. "But, yes. Yes, you can call a cab."

"I'll do it downstairs," Veronica said. "You don't have a book up here and information can be exasperating. The number's tacked on the bulletin board in the kitchen."

Anne thanked her, told her when she was due at the airport, and they hugged each other, stiffly, at first, and then with a rush of warmth. "I wish we could have gotten to know each other better," Veronica said.

"We still can," Anne said. "I'll let you know where I am. I'll want to hear how your ultimatum comes out. And . . . all the luck in the world, Veronica."

Veronica made an attempt at laughter. "We'll remember this as Independence Day. More than a month early."

"With no fireworks." Anne suspected they would not see each other again.

"Oh, there'll be fireworks," Veronica predicted. She walked to the door, then turned. She looked very small and very vulnerable, Anne thought. But, somehow, Anne suspected that she was going to make an important change in her life. "There'll be fireworks," Veronica repeated. "But isn't it about time?"

There were no members of the Delon family in sight when the butler, helped by Amalia and Guadalupe, carried Anne's luggage to the driveway. The taxi driver helped them load Anne's suitcases into the trunk of the cab. There were surprisingly tearful good-byes from the young maids. And then Anne was on her way, suspecting that Larry might be watching her departure from an upstairs window, but not looking back. Her heart felt heavy. *Evan.* Why had she spoiled everying with Evan? For a moment she was tempted to ask the driver to stop at Evan's house, but, remembering the coldness of their last parting, she lost her nerve.

The driver rounded the turn out onto the main road. Then, after driving several yards, he slowed down. Anne was shocked to see him turning into Evan Forrester's driveway.

"I'm going to Kahului," Anne protested. "To the airport."

"Yes, ma'am," The driver said. "But I got my orders to stop here."

"Orders? I'm the passenger," Anne insisted. "I don't want to . . ."

"Mrs. Delon told me what to do," the driver said. His fat brown face and expressive Hawaiian eyes were reflected in the rearview mirror. "They're good customers. I don't argue with Mrs. D, yeah?"

"I insist that you turn around!" Anne's heart was beating like a jackhammer. She moved to the edge of her seat. "Mrs. Delon doesn't give me orders about . . ."

It was too late. In the same instant that Anne recalled that Veronica's last name was Delon, too, she saw Evan standing at the edge of his driveway, his arms folded in front of him, looking toward the cab as though he had been expecting it.

"I drive her husband home enough when he gets too smashed to drive," the cabbie went on. "That lady tells me stop here, I stop here."

He stopped. And Evan hurried to open the back door. "You were actually leaving! Actually going away without so much as a fare-thee-well!" He was in one of his raging moods. "Come out here!" he ordered.

She was flustered by the unexpected meeting, still affected by the mere sight of Evan, yet not quite ready to respond to his command. "It's Independence Day," she said defiantly. Her voice quavered.

"Please don't argue," Evan said firmly. He turned to the driver, who had gotten out of the cab. "The lady's luggage, please, Kapono." Anne saw a folded bill pressed into the man's chubby hand. They seemed to know each other.

"Evan, I'm sorry I didn't stop to say good-bye," Anne argued. "I . . . I probably would have called you from the airport. But I'm going to miss my plane. I can't take another cab, and if you take my luggage out of the trunk . . ."

It was being unloaded by the driver as Anne spoke. "You might as well get out," Evan said in a grim voice. "You're not going to the airport. Not until I have a chance to talk some sense into you."

Her suitcases were being piled next to the driveway. Bewildered and shaking, Anne had no choice but to get out of the cab. Standing beside Evan, Anne watched as the driver made a mock salute, got behind the wheel and circled the driveway, on his way back to the road.

"You can't do this to me!" Anne cried. "Evan, I've been doing what other people want me to do ever since I came here. Now I'm finally making a decision of my own and . . ."

"It's the wrong decision," Evan said. "You've been making wrong decisions since before you got here." He closed one hand over her arm. "Let's go inside. I don't have any help around the place, but I'll come back for your luggage later. Unless you still want to leave. Unless you want to make another stupid, idiotic, senseless decision."

He was steering her toward the house, ignoring Anne's protests, taking long strides so that Anne had to take double steps to keep up with him.

Inside Evan's spacious living room, she was told to sit down. Half resentful, half excited, Anne hesitated.

"*Sit down!*" Evan's loud voice echoed through the room.

Anne sank down onto one end of a long white sofa. Evan nodded his approval, then dropped down beside her. Taking Anne's hand into his, talking to her as though she were a small child, he asked in a more gentle tone, "Exactly where did you think you were going?"

She had to admit that she'd had no specific

destination. Tears sprang up in her eyes. "Just . . . away," she said. "Just . . ."

"Someplace where you'd never have to see the Delons again?"

Anne nodded miserably.

"What about me, Anne? Didn't you ever want to see me again?"

She couldn't stop the tears from streaming down her face. "The way you talked . . . in the cabin . . . saying I was a fool and . . ."

"You really know so little about men, Annie. So little! Do you have any idea of how frustrated I was? To have gotten that close to you, then suddenly . . ." Evan made an incredulous motion with his head. "You're lucky you didn't get raped, you silly goose. You didn't, because . . . listen to this and listen carefully. *I love you!* And you were going to walk out of my life without . . . my God, if Veronica hadn't called and told me what you were about to do, I might have spent the rest of my life looking for you!"

Anne was stunned by the impassioned sound of his voice. Only a fool could doubt his sincerity. "You were so cold. And . . . and, beyond saying that you wanted me, you never . . . there was never any talk about . . . anything beyond maybe . . ." She caught a deep breath. "Maybe making love to me."

"And then tossing you aside? Did you really think that, Anne?"

"Well, you never . . ."

"I never asked you to marry me because you couldn't seem to recognize that you'd made a mistake. As long as you were wearing . . ." Evan stopped in midsentence. He lifted Anne's hand for a closer examination. ". . . you were wearing an engagement ring. Where is it now, Anne?"

She was crying harder now, the words bursting from her. "In Larry Delon's pocket, in the family safe, on his mother's dresser. I don't know where on earth it is and *I don't care!*"

For an instant, Evan was startled by the untypical outburst. Even Anne was surprised by her own vehemence. And then, with a joyous whoop, she was swept into Evan's arms, hugged so tightly that Anne thought her ribs would break. He was kissing away her tears, tender and ecstatically happy at the same time. After a while, as the kisses grew more insistent, the pressure of his lips demanding a warmer response from Anne, Evan gave one of his commands. "Put your arms around my neck!" Anne obeyed, drawing his head closer to hers, clinging to him, barely able to believe what was happening.

Entwined in each other's arms, with Anne's breasts pressed against the iron hardness of Evan's chest, they were lost in the rapture of heated kisses that inflamed them both, that promised a point of no return.

"Hold me," Anne whispered hoarsely. "Oh, Evan, please don't ever let me go. I . . . need your strength. I need you."

"You're always going to have me to lean on, darling," he promised. Evan lifted his lips from Anne's face, moving his head far enough from her so that she could see the passion in his dark eyes as they locked with hers. "You're going to marry me, Anne. Today, tomorrow, as soon as it can be arranged."

"You . . . aren't asking me," Anne said breathlessly.

"*Telling* you, darling. I don't want to waste any more time with your confusions. You're going to be my wife."

Anne nodded. Then she clasped Evan closer to her, holding his body against her own as though she were drowning and didn't dare let him go. His hands moved over every curve of her body, exploring, bringing her to a heated rush of ecstasy that made it impossible to resist the daring exploration of his fingers, the sudden motion that tore her blouse from her shoulders. Her body had slid down so that she was lying prone on the sofa, with the weight of Evan's muscular frame pinning her down. Anne closed her eyes, giving herself up to the burning tide that was sweeping over her. "Love me," she heard herself crying. "Oh, Evan, please love me. I love you so!"

His hands were pressing against the small of Anne's back, arching her body closer to him, when, abruptly, Evan let her go. He got up from the sofa, standing over her, his black eyes flashing. "What's wrong?" she cried. "Evan . . . what . . . ?" Aghast, she choked out the question: "Did you do that . . . just to humiliate me?"

He leaned down to plant a soft kiss on

Anne's forehead. "No, darling. No. To repay you for bringing me to this point last night and then turning me away? No. I'm just . . ." He sat down on the edge of the couch, breathing hard, but talking calmly and firmly as he looked into Anne's eyes. "I'm just trying to prove to you, darling, that I have every bit as much self-control as Larry Delon. You're going to be my bride. My virgin bride. Maybe tonight, certainly tomorrow night. And I want it to be right for you. I want it to be a beautiful experience, not just a . . . an uncontrollable moment of passion." His eyes looked misty, and Anne had never seen his always handsome face look more beautiful. Beautiful. Perhaps it was not the word usually used to describe a strong, virile male, but Anne could think of no other. If she had ever doubted that she loved him and that he was more than worthy of her love, that doubt was now erased. "I want it to be right for you, Anne."

"I'm . . . going to start crying again," Anne warned him.

"Not here, you won't," Evan said, smiling. "I'm taking you to a hotel." He got to his feet, totally in control again.

Anne sat up. "To a . . . hotel?"

Evan nodded. "Where you'll wait until I find out what it takes to get married on this island. There won't be a big fancy wedding, dearest. But there's going to be a fantastic honeymoon aboard the *Sapphire*."

She was trembling with a different kind of excitement now. "Where will we be going?"

Anne worked at the hopeless task of trying to adjust her torn blouse.

"Anywhere. Everywhere. I don't know." Evan was like a happy little boy, suddenly. "And then we'll . . . we'll come back here, of course."

Anne scowled. She was beginning to enjoy Evan's playful mood. "And live next door to . . ."

"Oh, the Delons only spend a few months of the year in that house. And we'll build a higher wall. One nobody can leap over." He laughed, reaching for Anne's hands and pulling her to her feet, then embracing her and swinging her around so that she was forced to hold on to him for support. "And if we don't get invited to any parties next door, it won't matter. We'll be busy with parties of our own. Just the two of us."

He let Anne's feet touch the ground and she teased, "But not tonight?"

"Maybe tonight," Evan said. "In the meantime, I don't want our gossipy neighbors getting any wrong ideas. You're getting out of here. But not for long."

They were holding hands as Evan walked Anne out to the driveway. Then, as Evan loaded Anne's luggage into his car, Anne looked toward the wall that separated his property from that of the Delons'. Should she feel sorry for Larry? Should she let Mrs. Delon know that she regretted all the trouble and expense that had gone into the wedding all of the Delons' friends would talk about for years? No. Larry had not been heartbroken. Maybe, like his mother, he was even relieved. There was only one member of that family Anne wanted to see again. In the meantime, breathing a small prayer that Veronica would be able to change the course of her life, Anne murmured, "Thank you, Mrs. Delon Junior."

Then, as Evan helped her into the small car, his touch warm and reassuring, Anne said, "I'm not going to like this, you know. A whole night alone in a hotel room . . ."

"Don't count on it," Evan said. He was smiling as he leaned down to kiss her. "I'm trying to be very noble, Mrs. Forrester."

"I'm not . . ."

"I'm just practicing. I like the way it sounds," Evan said. "I'm trying *very* hard to be a gentleman. But unless you go back into the house and change that ripped blouse, I won't be responsible."

They were both laughing as a suitcase was hauled out of the car and Anne went back to put on a top that wouldn't startle the room clerk in a hotel.

Evan waited for her outside. When, at last, they drove away from the house, Evan placed one hand on Anne's thigh, massaging her flesh under the thin skirt, assuring her that if there was a way to secure a marriage license and to find a minister who wasn't out surfing or sailing, she wouldn't be spending the night alone. Or any other night, for the rest of her life. "Cross your fingers and hope I find him," Evan said.

Anne crossed her fingers. She leaned closer to Evan, so that the firmness of his body would assure her that she was not dreaming. "Cross yours, too, Evan. I don't think I can wait."

Silhouette Special Edition

MORE ROMANCE FOR
A SPECIAL WAY TO RELAX

☐ 28579 6   **TERMS OF SURRENDER**   No. 1   95p
Janet Dailey

☐ 28580 X   **INTIMATE STRANGERS**   No. 2   95p
Brooke Hastings

☐ 28581 8   **MEXICAN RHAPSODY**   No. 3   95p
Diana Dixon

☐ 28582 6   **VALAQUEZ BRIDE**   No. 4   95p
Donna Vitek

☐ 28584 2   **SEARCH FOR A NEW DAWN**   No. 6   95p
Billie Douglass

*All these books are available at your local bookshop or newsagent, or can
be ordered direct from the publisher. Just tick the titles you want and fill
in the form below.*

Prices and availability subject to change without notice.

SILHOUETTE BOOKS, P.O. Box 11, Falmouth, Cornwall.

Please send cheque or postal order, and allow the following for postage
and packing:

U.K. – 40p for one book, plus 18p for the second book, and 13p for
each additional book ordered up to a £1.49 maximum.

B.F.P.O. and EIRE – 40p for the first book, plus 18p for the second
book, and 13p per copy for the next 7 books, 7p per book thereafter.

OTHER OVERSEAS CUSTOMERS – 60p for the first book, plus
18p per copy for each additional book.

Name ....

Address ....

....

Coming Next Month

Silver Mist by Sondra Stanford

Laurel Patterson ran away with her sister and niece to a small town in Texas to escape from a disastrous love affair. To finally free her mind from the painful memories, Laurel concentrates all her energy on setting up the child-care centre she and her sister are starting. Then Stephen Tanner, a local rancher, enters her world and proceeds to win over her sister and niece. Laurel slowly and unwillingly succumbs to his charms and irresistible manner. But now that Laurel has adjusted to the challenge of a new life and a new business, the hardest challenge of all is adjusting to a new man.

Texas Rose by Katharine Thiels

Alexis Kellogg's big breakthrough as a reporter brought her back to the town she had left in scandal—and into the arms of the man who drove her away. Cade Morse was one of the richest men in Texas and Alexis' job was to discover what drove him to the top. Was her destiny in his arms . . . or in the truth she was sent to unearth, the article she was compelled to write?

Never Give Your Heart by Tracy Sinclair

Gillian North was thrilled to land the Bliss Cosmetics account, but not with Bliss owner, Roman Barclay, who was determined to make Gillian part of the deal.

Then, quickly, things changed between them, and Gillian began to dream of a shared future. But the dream was shattered when Roman showed, unmistakably, just what she was to him: a prize possession, expensively bought.

She knew her heart was lost; could she salvage her pride?

Coming Next Month

Keys To Daniel's House by Carole Halston

Sydney Cullen had no use for men. All her energies went into her family and her career. The accusation that her looks were behind her success stung, and she grasped the chance to disprove the statement.

How could she have known that in using Daniel Bates to prove her point she would prove only that, no matter how hard she tried, she could never escape her own needs, her own passions?

All Our Tomorrows by Mary Lynn Baxter

Ex-tennis star Brooke Lawson's brother insists she recover from her crippling car accident at his home in Hawaii. Faced with the possible end to her career, Brooke struggles to regain her confidence and physical strength amidst her tormenting attraction to entrepreneur, Ashley Graham. Ashley, a hard-driving and virile man, arranges a marriage with her which she must accept to learn the depth of her passion for him. But can she continue a forced commitment to a man who demands all of her?

Love Is Surrender by Carolyn Thornton

Jennifer Waring, an attractive, young journalist, heartbroken over her divorce, felt like she belonged to another era as she drove down the treelined drive to the Esplanade plantation. She had been hired to publicize Esplanade and its owner, Ham Bertout. Ham relights the flame of desire within Jennifer, as she does in him. It is Jennifer's desire to do what is right and to be certain her love for her ex-husband is over that nearly destroys their new found love.